The party wars . . .

Elizabeth closed her textbook with a smack. "Don't even try to act like it's just some coincidence you're having your party on Friday night," she said angrily. "I'm sure you found out about our plans, and that's when you changed yours. It figures one of the requirements for being a Unicorn is having absolutely no morals!"

"We have plenty of molars—I mean, morals," I snapped back.

"Well, stealing our Friday night is a horrible thing to do!" Elizabeth shot back, tossing her pen onto the desk.

"Can we help it if we picked the same night as you?" I cried.

"Yes—you could change it," Elizabeth replied. "But you'd never do that. You're a Unicorn, and being a Unicorn means being nasty and unfair!"

"Is that so?" I could feel my heart pounding. "Well, if it's so horribly *awful* to be a Unicorn, then how come Mandy quit *your* boring, goody-goody club to come back to *ours!*"

Elizabeth's face fell. "I'm trying to study, so would you please go?"

I slowly turned around and walked out the door, my heart beating furiously. The fights between the Angels and the Unicorns in the past were pretty bad, but I had a feeling we hadn't seen anything yet. The real war was about to begin.

Bantam Books in THE UNICORN CLUB series.
Ask your bookseller for the books you have missed.

THE UNICORN CLUB™

ANGELS
KEEP
OUT

Written by
Alice Nicole Johansson

Created by
FRANCINE PASCAL

BANTAM BOOKS
NEW YORK • TORONTO • LONDON • SYDNEY • AUCKLAND

RL 4, 008-012

ANGELS KEEP OUT
A Bantam Book / May 1996

Sweet Valley High® and The Unicorn Club®
are registered trademarks of Francine Pascal

Conceived by Francine Pascal

Produced by Daniel Weiss Associates, Inc.
33 West 17th Street
New York, NY 10011

Cover art by James Mathewuse

ISBN: 0-553-48356-0
Published simultaneously in the United States and Canada

Bantam Books are published by Bantam Books, a division of Bantam
Doubleday Dell Publishing Group, Inc. Its trademark, consisting of the
words "Bantam Books" and the portrayal of a rooster, is Registered in U.S.
Patent and Trademark Office and in other countries. Marca Registrada.
Bantam Books, 1540 Broadway, New York, New York 10036.

PRINTED IN THE UNITED STATES OF AMERICA

OPM   0 9 8 7 6 5 4 3 2 1

To Gabriel Markowitz

One

"Jessica, can I have another graham cracker? *Please?*"

"Well . . ." I looked inside the box. I'd been eating so many crackers myself, I didn't know if any were left for the kids at the Sweet Valley Child Care Center, where my friends and I sometimes volunteer after school. "Oh—here's one!" I handed a broken piece to Gabriella, a five-year-old girl I'd been playing checkers with that afternoon.

"Is it just me, or does it seem like we've been running out of everything here lately?" Lila Fowler asked. She looked around the large playroom. "I mean, first there wasn't enough juice, then there weren't enough glasses—"

"And then Oliver spilled his juice, and we couldn't find anything to clean up the mess with," I added. Not to mention that Gabriella and I barely had enough checkers to play a full game.

Lila swept her long brown hair over her shoulder. "It's enough to make me ask Daddy to make another huge donation to this place. Only he's in Tokyo this week, and after that he goes straight to London for a bunch more meetings."

"Must be nice," I grumbled. Lila has been my best friend for years, and for as long as I've known her, she somehow manages to bring up the fact that she's disgustingly rich at *least* five times a day. Of course, it does just sort of come up—the same way my utter lack of money always comes up. At the *worst* times. Like after I've made it to the cash register with some new platform sandals I'm psyched to buy.

"Anyway, maybe there's something the Unicorn Club can do to help the Center get new supplies," Lila suggested.

"Good idea," I replied. My friends in the Unicorn Club and I have been volunteering at the Child Care Center in Sweet Valley ever since we got into trouble at school. (Never mind why. It's history now.) Our principal, Mr. Clark, sentenced us to volunteer at the Center for several dozen hours. We were all upset at first, but "punishment" turned out to be a good thing. We all love the kids at the Center—most of the time, anyway. So even when our official "sentence" was up, we decided to keep volunteering a couple afternoons a week.

"Let's definitely talk about it at our next meeting," Lila said.

"Which is at my house," I told her with satisfaction.

Lila rolled her eyes. "I *know* that, Jessica."

I grinned. One thing you should know about the Unicorns is that we're all really competitive with each other, and we kind of fight over who gets to host the meetings. Ellen Riteman hosts a lot of them, since she's our newly elected club president. Besides Ellen, Lila, and me, the club includes Mandy Miller and Kimberly Haver, the only eighth-grade Unicorn. The rest of us are in seventh grade together at Sweet Valley Middle School. Lila peered out the window. "I wonder where your mom is, Gabriella."

"Late, as usual," Gabriella said with a sigh.

"Don't worry—she'll be here," I said, smiling at the little girl. Then I turned back to Lila. "Aren't you just so glad that Mandy's back?" For a brief period of time, our friend Mandy Miller had deserted the Unicorns and joined another club. Not just any other club, but the Angels.

Just thinking of the Angels made me frown. Even though my twin sister Elizabeth is a member, and I love her to death, her *club* is another matter entirely.

Actually, for a little while, the girls who are now Angels were members of the Unicorn Club. That was before we realized those girls just aren't cut out to be Unicorns—they're way too goody-goody. Now, the only place the two clubs mix is the Center, since the Angels volunteer here, too.

"Yeah, well, of course Mandy came back," Lila said with a superior smirk. "I mean, how long was she supposed to resist being in the number-one club?"

Gabriella cleared her throat loudly.

"What is it?" I asked, concerned. "Is your mom here?"

Gabriella shook her head. "No . . ." she said slowly. "It's just that . . . well, I always thought the Angels were the number-one club at your school."

I stared at Gabriella, feeling as if I'd just been punched in the stomach. *The Angels? The best club? In what universe!* I felt like screaming. "You did? Why?" I asked her.

"I don't know." Gabriella shrugged. "I just thought that's what somebody said—like my older brother once."

"Your older *brother*?" Gabriella's older brother, Antonio, is a major hunk in the eighth grade. I turned to Lila. "Did I just hear what I think I heard?"

"Pretend you didn't," Lila replied, looking as horrified as I felt. How did such vicious rumors get started, anyway?

"Well, I guess I'll see you at school tomorrow," I said to Lila once the Fowler limousine had dropped me off in front of my house.

Lila nodded. "I love Fridays."

"Me too," I said. I hesitated, my hand on top of the door. "Lila, you know what? I've been thinking, and . . . maybe we should listen to Gabriella. Maybe she's right."

"Gabriella?" Lila asked, giving me a confused look. "Wait a second—what do you mean? Right about what?"

"About the Angels being the top club," I said, feeling dejected.

"What?" Lila practically yelled. She jumped out of the limousine and faced me. "Don't tell me you're thinking of leaving the Unicorns now, too!"

"No—never," I quickly reassured her. Had Lila lost her mind? "What I meant was, of course *I* don't think the Angels are the best club. But if *Gabriella* thinks they are, then we definitely have a problem on our hands."

"Gabriella's only five," Lila declared in a haughty tone. "She doesn't know anything."

"Yeah," I said slowly, "but if *she* thinks they are, then maybe other people do, too. Like . . . people at school. Including important people, and important *boys*."

"Oh." Lila stared off into space, as if the truth of what I'd just said was slowly dawning on her. "That would be horrible."

"Exactly," I agreed. Especially after we'd worked *months* to build our image at school. "I mean, who knows how these evil rumors get started, but once they do, it's our job—"

"Practically our social responsibility," Lila added.

"To stop them," I finished.

"Cold," Lila agreed. She tapped her chin with her finger. "But how?"

"I don't know how," I said. "But we'd better do something about it, before it gets out of control."

"We can talk about it at the meeting on Saturday," Lila said.

"At my house," I said again, starting to feel a

little better. We'd kill this rumor before it could do any real damage.

"Elizabeth! You've got to hear this!" I rushed into my sister's room that night. Sometimes she gets mad at me for not knocking, but come on—I don't have time to wait for her to say, "Come in," which she's going to do anyway, right? So what's the point? It's not like we keep secrets from each other—not usually, anyway.

Instead of sitting at her desk doing homework, like she usually is on any given school night, Elizabeth was examining herself in the mirror on her closet door.

"You have to listen to this song." I ran to Elizabeth's bedside table and turned on her clock radio. Music flooded the room. "It's my new favorite. Isn't it great?"

Elizabeth just shrugged. She had a dreamy expression on her face. "Yeah, it's fine."

"Fine? Try completely and utterly *hip*," I said. I glanced down at my sister's bed. An open notebook was lying on the end, by her pillow. *That figures*, I thought. Elizabeth is always writing something—either a story for the *7 & 8 Gazette*, the school newspaper, or a plot for a mystery novel, or—"Wait a second." I grabbed the notebook and grinned. "What is this?"

The notepaper was covered with words—actually, all the *same* word. *Todd*. In small letters, in capital letters, in print, in cursive . . . *Todd*.

"Hey, put that notebook down," Elizabeth cried, hurrying over.

I giggled and stared down at the sea of Todds. "I can't believe it. Mom and Dad always think you're up here studying—and look at this!"

"I—I *am* doing homework," Elizabeth sputtered in protest.

"Oh, sure," I said, nodding. "And I suppose this is a new course you're taking? Toddology? Todd Studies? Todd Language Arts?"

"Quit it!" Elizabeth demanded, grabbing the notebook out of my hand. She stuffed it into the top drawer of her desk and turned around to face me, arms folded across her chest.

"Well?" I said.

"Well what," Elizabeth muttered.

"Well, what's the big deal about Todd all of a sudden?" I stretched out on her bed, punching the pillows before laying down. I figured this ought to be good.

Elizabeth bit her lip. "Nothing."

"Ha!" I cried. "You're not going to pretend you didn't write all that. I'd know your handwriting anywhere. So what's going on?"

"Nothing!" Elizabeth insisted again.

"Uh-huh. Right," I teased her, rolling my eyes. "You keep saying that, but I know what I saw."

Elizabeth sighed. "Didn't you come in here to tell me about some song? You know, I didn't get to hear the whole thing, but what I did hear, I really liked."

"Don't change the subject." I sat up on the bed.

"Are you in love with Todd Wilkins or something?" My very own sister—in love! It was so exciting.

Only I have always thought I'd be the one to fall in love first. I spend a lot more time worrying and thinking about boys, so it would only be *fair*. Of course, I'm used to not getting what I deserve, like a huge allowance and a telephone in my room with my own private line.

"No, I am not *in love*," Elizabeth said in a disgusted tone. She made it sound as bad as having the flu or something.

"No, not at all," I said, trying to look serious. I shrugged. "You were just . . . checking your spelling, that's all. I think you've got it, Elizabeth. T-O-D-D. Of course, practice makes perfect, which must be why you wrote it down a hundred times. Not that you've ever had trouble with spelling before. In fact, didn't you win the spelling bee in fourth grade—"

"Stop it!" Elizabeth cried. Her face was turning as pink as my favorite lip gloss. "OK, so you caught me writing Todd's name. Maybe I was daydreaming about him a little. But that's it."

"Uh . . . huh," I said slowly.

"That's all!" Elizabeth repeated emphatically.

I got up from the bed. "There's a term for this, you know." I gave Elizabeth a sad, very sympathetic look. "Denial. Classic case of it."

"I'm *not* in denial," Elizabeth said, giggling.

"Oh, right. I can see that you're not," I said with a grin. "But if you ever need any advice on dating and love and that kind of thing? You know where to find me."

I stood up and walked out of her room, thinking over the situation. Of all the people for my sister to fall for, why Todd Wilkins? Sure he's cute . . . very cute. But his personality is about as exciting as a math quiz.

Then again, I wasn't surprised—Elizabeth and I don't have the same taste about much. That's one important reason why we aren't in the same club. The Unicorns are all about having a good time— going to parties, dancing, going out with boys, shopping. All the basic fun things. The Angels, on the other hand, like to sit around and think of ways they can help save the planet.

Not that I'm against saving the planet. Just not . . . every single minute of every day.

As I went back to my own room, I couldn't help feeling a little proud of Elizabeth for bucking the Angels' trend and actually thinking about a boy instead of her homework. Elizabeth has always called *me* boy-crazy—she obviously has never understood how it feels to really like a boy. This was kind of fun—now we actually have something in common besides our looks!

And the next time Elizabeth accused me of being boy-crazy? I could just pull that notebook out of her desk and settle *that* argument, once and for all.

Two

Todd.

It was lunchtime on Friday, and I could hear everyone around me talking, but I couldn't pay attention to what they were saying. I was too busy watching Todd. Watching him in line at the cafeteria, watching him sit down with his friends, watching him pick up his fork . . .

Stop it! I told myself. *This is ridiculous.*

But I couldn't help it. He is so cute, with his brown hair, his striped rugby shirt. I love the way he smiles. His whole face lights up when he laughs. He has a great laugh, too—not too loud, not too soft. . . . *Just right,* I thought.

Then I shook my head. *Who am I, Goldilocks all of a sudden?*

I turned to Mary Wallace, who was talking to the other Angels at our table, which we called the

Angeliner. Mary is the most sensible person I know. If I could just focus on what she was saying, I'd be able to forget about Todd.

"So then I said, 'Look, Mom, I can't clean my room *and* do all my homework, so you have to pick one,'" Mary was saying.

"So what did she pick?" Evie Kim asked. Evie lives with her mother and her grandparents, who moved to California from Korea.

"Homework, of course," Mary said. "That was the good news. The bad news is, she said I could clean my room tomorrow morning."

Maria Slater groaned. "I hate spending Saturday cleaning my room." Maria has long, curly dark brown hair and light brown skin. She had been a child actress in Hollywood when she was younger. "Saturdays are supposed to be for hanging out with friends!"

Saturday, I thought, blushing. I just remembered—I'd had a dream the night before about spending my Saturday with Todd!

In the dream, I'd woken up, gotten dressed, and gone downstairs to find Todd waiting for me, carrying a single red rose. "Today is Elizabeth Wakefield Day," he'd said with a smile. "We can do whatever you want to!" I took his hand, and we started dancing around the living room, which turned into the beach, and before I knew it, I had my arms around Todd and was about to kiss him!

I'd woken with a start, my alarm clock blaring. Why did I have to set that dumb alarm, anyway? If

I'd slept a few more minutes, maybe I could have actually kissed Todd.

But what was I thinking? It *was* just a dream. It didn't really count. Even if just remembering it did make my heart beat faster.

"What about you, Elizabeth? What are you doing on Saturday? Do you want to go for a bike ride or something?" Evie asked me.

I looked at her, a little startled. "Oh, I, uh, don't know. I mean, a bike ride sounds like fun." *It's just that my date with Todd sounds more fun.*

Evie looked at me curiously. "Are you OK? You look kind of—flushed or something."

My face felt hot. "Oh, yeah. I'm fine. I'm just— the lights in here are really bright, you know?"

I took a sip of my orange juice, not sure if I'd just made any sense at all. In a way, I wanted to tell the Angels what I was feeling, but somehow I just couldn't. They'd think I was being silly—just like a boy-crazy Unicorn or something. And it wasn't as if I actually had a real shot at going out with Todd. He didn't seem very interested in me. The few times we'd talked recently, he was busy concentrating on playing basketball or hanging out with his friends or working on his science project.

It was weird. Back in the sixth grade, we'd gone to some movies and dances together, and we always had a good time. We weren't really boyfriend and girlfriend, but we weren't just friends, either.

Now things were different—no dances and no movies. It figured. In seventh grade, you were too old to go to a dance with someone unless you were really dating him—and Todd and I definitely weren't doing that. In fact, from what I could tell, Todd didn't think of me as anything besides a friend.

It was definitely time for me to come back to earth and forget about my dream. Even though part of me didn't want to.

I smiled at Evie as brightly as I could. "You know what?" I said. "I think we ought to go try those bike trails over by the ocean—"

I broke off as an incredibly loud burst of happy laughter rang out across the cafeteria.

"I'd know that laugh anywhere," Maria said with a depressed sigh.

We all stared at the table where the Unicorns were sitting.

"Mandy looks like she's having a great time with the Unicorns," Evie commented sadly, resting her elbows on the table and gazing over at Mandy.

I nodded. Ever since Mandy had decided to quit the Angels and go back to being a Unicorn, our club just hadn't felt the same. Mandy is so funny, and she always has so much energy—not to mention the fact that she is the funkiest and best dresser at Sweet Valley Middle School. When she left the Angels, she created a big hole . . . one that my friends and I haven't been able to fill yet.

Not that Mandy and I aren't still friends, but it just isn't the same. We hardly spend any time together anymore.

"I can't believe she'd rather hang out with them,"

Maria said, shaking her head. "I mean, no offense to your sister, Elizabeth. She can be OK. But Lila? And Kimberly? They're so snotty!"

"Yeah, I know," I said. I'd been on the receiving end of their catty remarks a million times. Of course, Lila and Kimberly—and Ellen—aren't all bad. They'd do just about anything for Jessica. But if you asked me, that didn't make up for how mean and selfish they could be.

"Well, they certainly look like they're having fun," Mary said, slumping down in her chair.

I looked around the table. I'd never seen such a sad, pathetic-looking group in my life. "Come on, you guys—we can't mope about Mandy forever," I said. "And I know exactly what we need to make us feel better."

"What's that?" Evie asked, resting her cheek on her hand. "Chocolate cake?"

"No," I said with a smile. "But I guess I could make some brownies or something. How about if we have a club meeting and party tomorrow afternoon, at my house?"

"That sounds better than a bike ride," Evie said, sitting up a little. "Not that I don't love exercise, but . . . we're talking brownies."

"I can definitely come," Maria said.

Mary smiled. "Me too. My weekend just got a lot more interesting. Forget cleaning my room!" She crumpled her napkin and tossed it onto her tray. "So what time should we show up?"

I shrugged. "How about two o'clock? That way

we can hang out in the afternoon and I can try to talk my parents into letting us order a pizza for dinner."

"You know what I love about you, Elizabeth?" Mary smiled. "The fact that you'd think about ordering a pizza, like, *today*. You're always looking so far ahead."

I smiled back, but I couldn't help stealing glances at Todd, who was goofing off with his friends, playing football with a folded-up piece of paper. Why did he have to look so cute even when he was acting goofy?

I was perched on the edge of my backyard pool, my legs dangling in the cool water. I couldn't imagine a better way to spend my Saturday afternoon. Unless of course I was sitting at a pool in the south of France, being waited on by cute boys. . . .

"Boy, am I parched," Lila commented. "Jessica, I could really go for some more iced tea."

"Sure. It's in the fridge," I offered, tilting my face up to the sun.

Lila cleared her throat. "Hello, this *is* your house, isn't it?"

"Oh. I guess I should get it." I stretched my arms over my head and slowly stood up.

"Yeah, I *guess*," Lila said, adjusting the elastic band holding back her hair.

"Well, excuse me, but not all of us have maids!" I retorted. "I'm sorry if it takes me fifteen seconds to get into the house and back!"

"Come on, you guys—don't argue," Ellen

Riteman said. "We're having a meeting here as soon as Kimberly shows up, remember? And we have a big agenda to get through."

"Ellen's right," Mandy said. "No fighting! Unless of course it's over who gets to put sunscreen on my back." She stretched out on her stomach beside the pool. "By the way, Ellen, since when do you use the word *agenda*?" she teased.

"I've been reading a bunch of business books of my mom's," Ellen responded. "I mean, seeing as how I'm president and all. . . ."

"OK, Miss President." Mandy mock-saluted Ellen, who giggled.

"I'll get the iced tea." I sauntered slowly across the lawn and into the kitchen, hoping to irritate Lila just a little bit.

As I reached into the fridge for the iced tea, there was a knock at the back door. I walked over and opened it. "Oh, hi, Kimberly!"

"I thought I'd *never* get here," Kimberly said, striding into the house. She dropped her black-and-white-speckled bag onto a chair. "I had to do about a million errands with my mother. Like *grocery* shopping."

"Ugh," I said. Kimberly had just moved back to Sweet Valley after living in Atlanta for a few months. She can be a little on the bossy side, but I like her take-charge attitude. Most of the time, anyway. Kimberly is a terrific horseback rider, and she keeps up on every trend there is, all over the world.

"I hate shopping for food," I continued. "Too

bad it's practically required if you plan on eating anywhere besides the Dairi Burger."

"Well, when I grow up, I'm having my groceries delivered," Kimberly said.

"Oh, yeah? Well, I'm having my . . . chef pick them up," I said, giggling. I took a glass out of the cupboard for Kimberly, and we walked back outside to the pool.

"OK, Kimberly's here! Time to get this meeting started!" I announced. "We have some very important business to discuss."

"Right," Ellen said, shifting in her lounge chair. "I now officially call this meeting to order."

Kimberly sat down next to her. "So what's the important business?"

"It's something that Jessica and Lila want to discuss. So I turn the floor—or patio, rather—over to you guys." Ellen giggled.

I poured some iced tea over the ice cubes in Lila's glass. "OK. Here's the deal. Lila and I heard something that made us think that what other people think of us isn't what we'd want them to think, and so we need to do something to make them think the way we think."

Mandy stared at me. "Huh?"

Lila shook her head. "What Jessica means is, we're afraid that some people at school . . . and around town . . . might have the wrong *idea* about us." She gave me a pointed look. "Is that more clear?"

I rolled my eyes. If you asked me, it was perfectly clear the way I'd said it.

"For instance, we were talking to Gabriella down at the Center," Lila continued, "and she happened to let it slip, somehow or other, that she didn't know the Unicorns are the best club."

Kimberly gasped. "You're kidding!"

I nodded. "And it gets worse. She actually thinks that the Angels are a better club than—"

Kimberly held up her hands. "Stop right there. I don't want to know anything else." Kimberly had more against the Angels than anyone else. For some reason she just can't stand them—I guess because she knows they don't like *her*, and she doesn't like most people who don't think she's great. Anyway, she stood up and started pacing around the patio. "OK, so what you guys are saying is, we have a public-relations problem."

"I get along with the public just fine!" Ellen said defensively.

"What she means is, people aren't perceiving us the way we want them to," Mandy explained to Ellen.

"Oh." Ellen cleared her throat. "Right."

I looked at my friends seriously. "And what we need is—"

"A plan," Kimberly broke in. "We need to let people know who we are. We have to show them that the Unicorns are the top club at Sweet Valley Middle School. And the easiest way to do that is . . ." She hesitated, her brow wrinkled in concentration.

"We could advertise ourselves!" Ellen suggested. "We could rent a billboard and put our pictures on it."

"And then what? Say, 'Call 1-800-UNI-CORN'?" Mandy laughed.

"Well," Ellen said, looking offended. "At least I made a suggestion."

"True. And advertising's not completely off track," Lila said. "I mean, my father says it works wonders for his company."

"Yeah, but the difference between us and your father is that he has a huge budget for advertising," Mandy argued. "As in, millions of dollars. We, on the other hand, have about twenty-five cents. We need *free* advertising."

"What if we got an article written about us?" I said, thinking of all the articles Elizabeth writes for the school newspaper. "Free publicity—that's what it's called, right?"

"Yeah, but to get free publicity you have to actually do something," Mandy pointed out. "And we're not exactly planning to do something amazing to help save the world, are we?"

"Yes, we are!" Kimberly suddenly cried.

"We are?" I asked. "Wait—are we going to give free fashion makeovers at school again?" Making everyone look better *can* be kind of like saving the world.

"No, nothing like that!" Kimberly said, shaking her head. "This is way better." Her eyes sparkled. "We're going to have a *party!* A *huge* party. One that everyone at school will come to, and when they leave, after having a great time, they'll all *know* who the best club at school is."

Now that was more like it! I love parties. Of any

size. For any cause. But the bigger, the better! "Kimberly, you're a genius," I said. "That is the perfect way to get our premier image back."

"I like it, I like it," Mandy said, nodding. "It's not exactly saving the world, but I guess if it makes the world a better place to live, at least for one night . . ." She shrugged. "How could anyone say no to that?"

"What about you guys?" Kimberly said, turning to Lila and Ellen.

Lila raised one eyebrow. "Have I ever said no to any party at any time?"

Ellen laughed. "I think that sounds great. Where should we have it? What kind of party should it be?"

"How about an outdoor party, so we'll have room for as many people as possible. . . ." Kimberly tapped her chin. "And let's see. Something casual, so everyone feels they can just sort of drop by and it's no big deal."

"How about a barbecue?" I suggested. "We could have it right here! We'll make tons of good food, and have dancing, and there's always the pool." I swept my hand in a wide arc, like a game-show assistant. "All this could be yours!"

Ellen giggled. "That sounds good."

Kimberly surveyed the yard, looking thoughtful. "A little on the simple side, but it ought to work."

"We can make it work," Lila declared. "I can see it now." She made a square with her fingers, pretending she was looking through a video camera. "Tons and tons of people in this yard, talking, laughing, dancing—I give it two thumbs up."

"This is a great backyard for a party," Mandy agreed. "We can get some of those strings of lights shaped like chili peppers and hang them on the back fence—"

"And my dad happens to be fantastic at making barbecued chicken," I said, my mouth watering at the idea. Anything with barbecue sauce on it is heavenly, as far as I'm concerned.

"I'll bring all my CDs," Lila added.

"And I'll make invitations on my computer," Kimberly said. "My dad's got this great new desktop publishing program. I can make up something really cool and then print enough copies for everyone at school."

Mandy cleared her throat. "Speaking of invitations . . ." She fiddled with the strap on her sandal.

"What? Did you want to do them?" Kimberly asked.

"No," Mandy said. "It's not that. I mean, of course I'd be happy to help. But . . ."

"But what?" I asked. "Spit it out already!"

"I was just wondering. If we're inviting everyone at school . . ." She looked up at me and shrugged. "Does 'everyone' include the Angels?"

"Oh." Kimberly made a face. "Well, I'm sure we can find some way around that."

"It's not like they'd want to come, so there's no point in inviting them anyway," Lila said. "Right?"

"I don't know." Mandy sighed. "It just seems pretty rude not to invite them. I mean, they are still my friends."

Not to mention my twin sister, I thought, glancing up at Elizabeth's bedroom window. I couldn't exactly exclude her from a party at her very own house. Besides, if inviting the Angels would make Mandy happy, it was better to go along with her. The last thing we wanted was for her to drop us for the Angels again!

"I think Mandy's right," I said. "We *should* invite the Angels."

Kimberly looked like she was about to protest. "Well . . ."

"Great!" Mandy burst out before Kimberly could say another word. "I was hoping you'd see it my way."

"Of course we do!" Lila said quickly. "If you think it's the right thing to do, Mandy, then we think it's the right thing to do." I could tell she was just as determined as I was not to offend Mandy.

"All right." Kimberly sighed. "We'll invite the Angels. Only I *hope* they realize what a humongous favor we're doing them. And if they don't? I have no problem reminding them," she said with a superior smile.

Three

"How does this look?" I held up an old red sweater, a black-and-white-checked miniskirt, and a pair of black pumps. I was trying to come up with an outfit to wear to school on Monday. I hadn't told the other Angels why I cared so much what I wore, but if I saw a good opportunity, I was going to bring up my massive crush on Todd.

The thought of telling them still made me nervous. I didn't want to jinx any chance I had with Todd. But keeping my feelings all to myself was too hard!

"Umm . . . that's not exactly the look you want, Elizabeth," Evie said, sounding a little uncomfortable. "Try the chunkier black shoes."

"And maybe another sweater," Maria recommended.

"And definitely another skirt," Mary added, making a face.

I dropped the clothes onto the floor and sank onto my bed. "We're hopeless."

"Yeah, I know," Mary agreed, sitting on the floor and leaning back against the bed.

"Without Mandy around, we might as well try to coordinate paper bags." Evie sat down next to Mary.

Maria stretched out on the floor, lying on her stomach. "Why did she have to quit, anyway?"

I hung my arms over the edge of the bed. Then we all simultaneously reached into the center of our circle and grabbed another butterscotch brownie off the plate I had put there.

I took a big bite, staring at the floor. "I guess we're not in the party mood after all." I sighed.

Maria chewed slowly, gazing dismally at the now empty plate. "There's no reason we should feel so bad. We're still a great club, even without Mandy."

"I know," I agreed. "It's just that I feel like something's missing."

"Me too," Evie said. "And it's called our *pride*."

"What do you mean?" Mary asked, brushing a crumb off her lip.

"Well, it's like we just don't feel like much of a club now that Mandy ditched us for the Unicorns," Evie said. "I mean, they have five people now, we have four—"

"But numbers don't count," I argued.

"I don't know," Maria said slowly. "I hate to say it, but I kind of agree with Evie. It's like I feel . . .

inferior or something, compared to the Unicorns."

I gazed at the plate on the floor, considering. I'd never thought of it in those terms, exactly. I was bummed that Mandy left us for the Unicorns, too, but did that make us inferior?

I could hear the Unicorns making a lot of noise outside. Jessica shrieked something to Lila, and Lila howled with laughter. They were definitely having a lot more fun than the Angels were, at least this afternoon. Then again, they had fun doing things that I didn't consider fun at all. Like gossiping and shopping and . . . boy watching.

Suddenly I felt my cheeks heat up as I remembered how I'd stared at Todd all through lunch on Friday. But now wasn't the time to think about him.

"OK, so maybe right now we all feel a little down," I said quickly. "But it's not like we'd want to *be* in the Unicorns with Mandy!"

"Oh, no," Maria said, looking at me as if I were crazy.

Mary shook her head. "Not in a million years."

"I don't even like purple," Evie declared in a snobby voice. "It looks terrible on everybody!"

I burst out laughing. One of the Unicorns' rules was to wear something purple at all times. Jessica had a million purple hair elastics stuffed into her locker at school for the days she forgot to dress correctly.

"Can you imagine being a Unicorn?" Maria said with a giggle. "You'd have to shop constantly, in between trashing other people and having crushes on a daily basis."

"It's like a full-time job!" Mary said. "I mean, having crushes all the time is *so* ridiculous."

I squirmed uncomfortably on the bed. "Well, crushes aren't so awful," I said softly. "I mean, it's perfectly natural and all to have a crush on someone."

"Sure, occasionally," Evie said with a wave of her hand. "But you can't think about boys constantly."

"You can't?" I said.

Evie and Mary stared at me as if I'd just said that I was really a frog instead of a human being.

I cleared my throat, laughing nervously. "I mean, no, of course you can't. It's like . . . you'd never get anything else done." Like your homework, for instance. I was already three days behind in history.

"Exactly," Maria agreed. "And crushes aren't such a hot idea anyway—you're too in the clouds most of the time, and you just end up getting hurt."

"You do?" I said, mulling that over. This wasn't sounding very promising.

"Oh, yeah," Maria said, nodding. "Crushes almost never work out."

"Never?" I asked, feeling my heart sink. Maria made it sound as if my life were about to be ruined if I kept liking Todd.

"I bet right now the Unicorns are sitting around the pool talking about boys and deciding which boy they'll ask to the senior prom in five years," Mary predicted.

"Really." I laughed uneasily. Was it so incredibly wrong to want to talk about boys? Or boy, singular?

"It's fine for them. But the thing I don't get is how Mandy can be so shallow," Evie mused. "I don't understand."

I don't understand, either, I thought. *But if liking boys is shallow, then . . . I'm not as deep as I thought I was.* I didn't know what was making me feel worse: Mandy deserting us for the Unicorns, or the fact that I was turning into one with my huge crush on Todd. Whichever it was, I decided it definitely wasn't a good time to tell my friends about my feelings for Todd. And I had to change the subject of boys and crushes, fast, before I let my true feelings slip.

"Well, we can't let Mandy's leaving get us down forever," I told everyone. "We have to start thinking of things that focus on . . . the future, instead of the past!"

"OK, Miss Self-Help," Mary teased me. "And just how do you propose we do that?"

"That's the part I'm not so sure about," I admitted. "But we'll think of something. I don't plan on feeling like this for the rest of the year!"

"Good thing, too," Maria said, pointing at the empty plate in front of us. "We can't keep devouring brownies like this every time we get together, or we'll have to call ourselves the Angel Food Cake Club instead of the Angels."

Evie laughed. "So, Elizabeth. Was that the last of the brownies—or are there more downstairs?"

I grinned and swung my legs to the floor. "Oh, I'm not sure. There might be a *few* left."

Everyone jumped up, scrambling for the door.

"Go, Angel Food Cake Club!" I shouted as we chased each other down the stairs.

"Mom?" I was in the kitchen Saturday night, helping my mother prepare cheese enchiladas for dinner. The other Angels and I hadn't felt much like ordering a pizza after eating brownies all afternoon. I was wondering how I'd manage to eat even one enchilada. "Have you ever felt like maybe . . . you didn't quite measure up?"

My mother turned around from the refrigerator, carrying a jar of hot spicy salsa. "Since when did you feel like that?"

"Since Mandy quit the Angels," I admitted shyly. "We all feel kind of like losers or something."

"That's ridiculous," my mom said. "I know for a fact that Mandy still likes and cares about each of you. She just felt like making a change, that's all. And she has a long history with the Unicorns."

"I know that," I said, turning on the oven and setting the temperature. "But I don't always *feel* that."

Mom nodded, brushing a strand of blond hair off her face. "I know what you mean. Well, what you guys need is to do something fun as a club, something that makes you all feel good."

"Right," I said. "But what? I mean, unless we could go four ways on a lottery ticket and win a million dollars every year for life. . . ."

"Actually, I was thinking that a party might be a good idea," my mother replied. "You could have it here—we have plenty of room, both inside and out. I'm sure your dad would be glad to fire up the barbecue. You could invite all your friends from school and—"

"Mom! That's exactly what we need!" I wiped my hands on a dish towel and threw my arms around my mother's waist. "It's totally perfect!" A party would give the Angels a project to work on together, and it was an instant way to make us all feel more popular. *And I can invite Todd—to my house!* I realized happily. Maybe that was the best reason of all to have a party.

Stop it, Elizabeth. You sound just like Jessica! I told myself. I felt like I was developing a split personality: half Angel, half Unicorn. Pretty strange to picture, isn't it?

"This is going to be great," I said, finally releasing my mom. "Do you think we could have it in the next week or so? The sooner the better. There's nothing like a party to cheer people up and . . . oh, my gosh, there's so much to *do*."

My mother grinned. "And since you're having the party here—where you and Jessica both live, if I'm not mistaken—this would be the perfect opportunity for the Angels and the Unicorns to mend fences."

I raised my eyebrows. *Mend fences? How about walls?* Anyway, the whole point of the party was to show everyone the Angels didn't need the Unicorns— or Mandy—to make us a cool club. Having the Unicorns around would spoil the whole thing. "Well, I'll have to talk to Jessica first," I said.

Since the party would be at my house, the least I

could do was invite my very own twin. Not that Jessica would be caught dead at any Angel party. I could picture her reaction now: "I'd rather write a book report—on *War and Peace!*"

But there was no harm in inviting her . . . as long as she didn't actually show up. Whenever the Unicorns are around, they always manage to cause trouble—and that was the last thing we needed at our party.

"So, I have some totally exciting news," I said at dinner Saturday night as I spooned enchilada sauce all over my plate. I was absolutely starving. "The other Unicorns and I were talking today, you know? And we decided—"

"You're all going *brunette* for fall," my older brother, Steven, broke in. "Oh, that *is* totally exciting, Jess!" he squealed.

I frowned at him. Did Steven have to make fun of me every single day of his life? "Aren't you supposed to be eating dinner at the food court or something? You know, table for one?"

Steven just smiled at me. "You were saying? Something about the Unicorns? Ooohhh, I can't wait to hear."

"Just ignore him," my father suggested as he helped himself to a tortilla chip. "Now, what's the news?"

"Well," I said, sitting up straighter in my chair. "We've decided it's time to have a party. A big party, for everyone at school. We're thinking

Saturday. Or if that's too soon, then the next weekend. And with you guys' permission, we want to have it right here!"

"Save me," Steven muttered.

"What?" Elizabeth demanded at the same time.

I looked at my sister. "I said, we'd like to have our party here, like next weekend or something."

"But that won't work at all," Elizabeth said.

"It won't?" I asked. "Actually, I think it's going to be pretty easy to set up, and—"

"No," Elizabeth interrupted me. "It's not that—I mean, it's a really good idea and all. It's just that . . . I'm already planning a party here for next weekend, with the Angels."

"What?" I exclaimed. "But—that's impossible!"

"Actually, I already asked Mom and she said it was fine," Elizabeth replied. "I'm really sorry, Jessica. I guess you guys will have to make another plan."

"You guess? You guess?" I felt my ears burning, and it wasn't from the extra-hot salsa I'd just eaten. There was something very funny going on. Only I didn't feel like laughing! "There's no way you guys came up with the same idea as we did by accident, Elizabeth. Because we were all sitting out by the pool this afternoon talking about it, and your window was open, and you were right above us, and I bet you guys all crowded around the window, listening to our conversation—"

"Excuse me, but we have better things to do at our meetings than listen to you guys!" Elizabeth broke in, frowning. "Anyway, it wasn't even my idea to have a party here. Mom was the one who suggested it," she said with a shrug.

"Mom?" I slowly turned and stared at my mother. "Mom? Is that true?"

She nodded. "I had no idea you were planning the same thing."

Betrayed by my very own mother! Isn't there a myth about this, or a TV movie or something? "Well, I don't buy that for one second. I'm sure Elizabeth suggested it first. Anyway, the Angels never have good ideas on their own. They've been copying us forever."

"C-copying you? Why would we want to copy you?" Elizabeth sputtered. "We don't even like the same things!"

"Go, Elizabeth! Go, Jessica!" Steven chanted, grinning from ear to ear. "Now this is what I call family entertainment."

"OK, everyone—that's enough," my father said, sounding very serious. "Let's all calm down and try to eat in peace. I'm sure there's a solution to this problem."

"Sure—it's simple. The Angels can cancel their party!" I said triumphantly.

"No way," Elizabeth replied coldly, glaring at me across the table.

"Listen, I have an idea," Dad said with a big smile. "Why don't the Angels and the Unicorns host this big party *together*?"

Elizabeth and I both turned and stared at him. I couldn't believe he'd even mentioned something so ludicrous. Was he totally ignorant of the facts? Was he living in another universe?

"Dad, I don't *think* so," I said, flipping my hair over my shoulder.

"Definitely not!" Elizabeth agreed.

I'd hardly ever heard her sound so rude before. There was something about the feud between our clubs that really got to both of us. In my opinion, Elizabeth and the other Angels ought to consider themselves lucky to even be invited to our party—much less co-host it! But Elizabeth made it sound as if she'd rather slice onions. Fine. I certainly didn't have to burden her with an invitation now!

"You know what? I have a better idea," I said.

"Cancel the party!" Steven cried. "Don't let them anywhere near our house! Please, Mom and Dad, I beg of you!" He looked desperately at my parents.

"No. We'd never cancel our party," I declared. "We'll just move it, that's all. We'll find someplace *better* to have our party." I cast a superior glance at Elizabeth.

"There's a better place than here? I think I'm offended," my dad joked.

"One down, one to go!" Steven said, pumping his fist in the air. "Yes!"

I crumpled my napkin and tossed it onto the table. "May I please be excused? I have a party to plan for next Saturday night." I looked at Elizabeth as I stood up from my chair. "A big party."

"But, Jessica—you've barely eaten," my mother protested, pointing to my plate.

"I'll eat later. Right now I have more important things to do!" Like show Elizabeth and the other Angels what happens when they steal our ideas!

Four

"You're kidding. She actually eavesdropped and stole our idea?" Kimberly asked me on Monday at lunch.

"That is so outrageous," Lila said. "I never thought Elizabeth would sink that low."

"Yeah, that doesn't sound like her," Mandy agreed.

I felt a little twinge of guilt. I had to admit, Mandy had a point. My sister isn't exactly the eavesdropping type. Still, whether the Angels meant to steal our party idea or not, the simple fact was—they'd stolen it. "Well, we *were* being kind of loud, I guess, and her bedroom window *is* right over the patio."

Ellen stirred her yogurt thoughtfully. "We'll have to meet someplace else next time we plan something important."

Kimberly nodded. "I'll say. The idea of them

using our idea . . . it's ridiculous!" She frowned at the Angels' table. "I ought to go over there right now and give them a piece of my mind."

"Don't do that," I said nervously. I could just see Kimberly picking a fight with Elizabeth in the middle of the cafeteria, and I definitely didn't want that to happen. And somehow it was seeming more and more unlikely that Elizabeth had actually done anything wrong. "I mean . . . we don't have time for that, because we need to spend our lunchtime figuring out where to have our party now. Oh, and get this—at one point, my dad actually suggested that the way to solve our little problem was to have a party *together*."

"Together? With them?" Kimberly scoffed. "Yeah, like that would happen!"

"In their dreams," Lila added, rolling her eyes. "Their party's probably going to be a total snooze, while ours, on the other hand—"

"Major excitement," Ellen said with a smile. "No, we could never co-host a party. It's against the law of nature or clubs or something!"

"Well, I don't think it's really all *that* ridiculous," Mandy said softly, fidgeting with her straw.

I bit my lip. Mandy didn't look offended exactly, but she did look kind of bummed out. "Umm, not that there's anything really *wrong* with the Angels," I said quickly. "I just think our parties should be separate, that's all. I mean, the Unicorns need our own distinctive reputation, right?"

"I guess so," Mandy replied, smiling a little.

"Well." Lila sniffed. "The Angels can have their

little party at your house, Jessica. We'll have ours at my house!" Her eyes twinkled. "It's a much better place, anyway, with our huge party room and everything."

"That sounds great!" Ellen cried. "Your mansion is so totally awesome—"

"Everyone's going to be really impressed," Kimberly said, grinning. "Good thinking, Lila. Your mansion's a much better place for a party."

My shoulders slumped. Did they have to go around insulting my house? "Look, I know my house isn't huge, but it's pretty nice, considering my parents aren't, like, hotshot millionaire studio executives or whatever. It wouldn't be so awful to have a party there."

"No, of course not." Kimberly put her hand on my arm. "I didn't mean it like that."

"Yeah, I love your house," Ellen said. "It's just that Lila's house has lots of advantages."

"Such as?" I asked.

"Such as a chef, a maid, and anything else we'd need," Lila said. "Including additional servants to do all the work. . . ."

"Hmm," I grumbled. I hated to admit it, but everyone was right: If Lila had the party, it would mean a lot less work for me. I'd be able to relax and focus on more important things, like what to wear and who to invite. "Well, OK," I relented. "Lila's house sounds all right."

"Think of it this way, Jessica," Kimberly said. "Compared to our huge shindig at Lila's mansion, the Angels' party is going to be like a little kid's birthday party!" she predicted. "Gee, I wonder if they'll get a *clown*."

I giggled. Maybe we were being a little overly competitive, but Kimberly had a point. When the Unicorns set out to prove something, we prove it in a big way. We are the number-one club at Sweet Valley Middle School, and after our party, nobody would ever forget it!

I glanced across the cafeteria at my sister. *Sorry, Elizabeth. But that's the way it has to be!*

"You're not Jessica," Oliver Washington said as soon as I walked into the Child Care Center on Monday afternoon. Oliver is kind of Jessica's special friend; they hit it off from the day she started volunteering at the Center. He loves Jessica so much, it's really cute watching them together.

"You're right, Oliver—I'm not Jessica. Sorry about that." Grinning at him, I set my backpack full of books on the floor. "But isn't it cool that you can tell us apart now?"

"Yeah. But I still want to see Jessica," Oliver said glumly, arms folded across his chest.

"Jessica doesn't come on Mondays, remember?" Mandy said. "She'll be here tomorrow, though, OK? Now come back and help me, Oliver—I'm terrible at this!" Mandy was sitting on the playroom floor, helping some kids build a giant tower of blocks. Oliver scooted back into the group and immediately started adding blocks to the tower.

"Hi, Mandy," I said, feeling a little uneasy about seeing her.

"Hey, Elizabeth. Give me a hand," Mandy said, glancing up at me with a smile.

I stepped closer to the circle on the floor. "Hi, everyone! How's it going?"

Nobody answered. They were all too busy concentrating on their tower.

"Well, I can see I haven't lost my touch," I joked to Mandy. I sat down on a metal folding chair next to the circle.

Mandy laughed nervously. "They're just preoccupied," she said. "Don't sweat it." She looked up at me again. "So. How's it going with you?"

I shrugged. "Fine. OK." I couldn't believe how awkward I felt around Mandy. I hated feeling that way, especially when we'd been such close friends. Somehow I had to break the ice. "Look, Mandy, I—"

"Elizabeth, I don't—" Mandy began at the same time.

I smiled. "You go first."

"No, you," Mandy said.

"OK." I took a deep breath. "I was just going to say that I wish things didn't have to be so weird between us. I mean, just because we're not in the same club anymore . . . that doesn't mean we can't still talk sometimes. Right?"

"That's exactly what I was going to say." Mandy smiled sheepishly. "I hate that we have to act like enemies. All this club stuff gets a little too serious sometimes. You'd think we were running for office or something."

"I agree!" I said with a laugh. "Clubs are important. But friends are important, too."

"I guess we all forget about that sometimes." Mandy sighed, putting a block on the stack. "I mean, we can get all caught up in doing stuff as a club. Like planning this huge, major party."

"I know what you mean," I responded. "It's kind of funny that we both came up with the same idea. I guess that means we're more alike than anyone wants to accept!"

"So great minds think alike and all that?" Mandy suggested.

"Something like that," I agreed, laughing. "Sure."

"Well, I personally think it's kind of stupid to have two separate parties," Mandy said. "But I guess that's what's going to happen."

"It'd be nice if you could come to our party," I told her. "I know everyone would want to see you."

Mandy smiled. "Well, I *would* like to come, but—"

"Maybe you could," I broke in excitedly. Just because we had separate parties didn't mean *we* had to stay separate. "It's going to be Friday night at seven o' clock at our house—if you have time, maybe you can drop by. You don't need to RSVP or anything."

"Well . . . I do want to," Mandy said, sounding hesitant. "But . . . other people might not like it if I do. I mean, I might have to help prepare for our party for most of the night."

"True," I said. "Well, just see how you feel. No pressure."

"What? No pressure? But—I can't *live* without pressure!" Mandy cried, waving her arms enthusiastically in the air.

The carefully constructed tower of blocks crashed to the ground.

"Mandy!" several voices yelled at once.

"Uh-oh," Mandy said, glancing at the five angry kids surrounding her. "Something tells me we're about to have more problems than planning our social lives!"

"How much will it cost to fix that?" I heard Mrs. Willard, the director of the Child Care Center, say into the phone. I was standing outside her office, waiting to mention to her that we were down to our last box of graham crackers and that we'd need more to last through the week.

"What?" Mrs. Willard continued. "But that's impossible! Well, we're a nonprofit organization. We don't have that kind of money!"

I winced. Mrs. Willard's usually so clearheaded that she's the one who calms *us* down, but now she seemed really rattled.

"That's ridiculously expensive. Don't you have a special rate to help organizations like ours? Oh. Well, I see. Thank you very much." She hung up the phone with an abrupt click and let out a deep sigh.

I hurried away down the hallway before Mrs. Willard could see me. I had a feeling she had enough big problems on her mind without worrying about graham crackers. Maybe I could pick up a couple of boxes and bring them over tomorrow, *then* tell her we'd need some soon. It would be less of an emergency that way.

I pushed open the front doors of the Center and started walking down the sidewalk toward home, thinking about Mrs. Willard's phone conversation. I'd noticed that a lot of things around the Center were in need of some repair. And we'd run out of some basic supplies lately, too—not just graham crackers. We were going to have to get some emergency funds soon to make it through the year OK without cutting services. *Maybe there's a way I could help. Maybe the Angels could—*

"Elizabeth! Hi!"

I practically fell over. It was Todd, riding up behind me on his mountain bike! "Hi!" I said, trying to ignore the nervous flutter in my stomach. "Umm . . . where are you going?"

"Oh, I was just riding around the neighborhood on my way home from the beach." Todd braked his bicycle and climbed off, standing beside me. He was wearing soccer shorts, a T-shirt, and sandals, and he had a beach towel hanging around his neck. In other words, he looked totally cute, as usual. "What about you? What's up?" he asked me.

"I'm on my way home from the Child Care Center," I said, quickly adjusting the ribbon in my hair. I'd been wanting to invite him to our party all day, but I hadn't gotten up the nerve. Now was the perfect opportunity—we were all alone. But being all alone was scary, too.

"Cool. We can walk together," Todd said.

I smiled at him. Why was he being so nice to me? Most boys I know wouldn't be caught dead walking a girl anywhere, much less to her house. I knew I ought to feel incredibly happy—and I *was* happy. But I was also completely tongue-tied. I knew I had to invite him, but I couldn't think of what to say!

Don't be silly, I told myself. *You've talked to Todd a hundred times before. Just start a conversation and work your way up to the invitation. Say anything!* "Nice weather, isn't it?" I blurted out, then cringed. *Anything but that!*

"Yeah. The beach was perfect," Todd replied. "Hot, but not too hot."

"I hope it stays nice all week," I said. I stole a quick glance at him. He was swinging his arms a little, and he had a small smile on his face. He didn't seem nervous or uncomfortable at all. *Just do it,* I told myself. *Ask him now!* "I'm having—I mean, umm, the Angels are having this . . . outdoor party Friday night," I said. "At my house."

"That sounds fun," Todd commented, adjusting the towel around his neck.

"Yeah, umm, actually, I was hoping I'd see you at school today, because I . . . wanted to invite you." My voice sounded so shaky, I barely even recognized it. "Will you come to my party?"

Todd's smile widened. "Sure! What time did you say?"

"I—I didn't say." I laughed nervously.

"That must be why I didn't know," Todd said. He grinned at me in a teasing kind of way, his brown eyes sparkling.

When I looked into his eyes, it was hard to remember that things like clocks and time zones even existed. "Uh . . . I think seven o'clock," I said, forcing myself to look away. "It's going to be a barbecue, with outdoor games and music."

"Seven." Todd nodded. "OK, then. It's a date."

I stopped dead in my tracks, staring at the ground and feeling like I was about to faint. Had I heard Todd right? Had he said "a date"? *A date!* He'd actually called it a date!

"Is something wrong?" Todd asked, giving me a confused look.

"Oh, no!" I said. "I just thought I saw a . . . ladybug, that's all, and I didn't want to umm . . . step on it. No, everything's fine." I smiled at him and continued walking down the street beside him.

Everything was better than fine—it was fantastic! I had a real date with Todd!

Five

"This is the best pasta salad I've ever had," Kimberly said on Monday night. We were all digging into a gourmet dinner at Lila's, trying to decide on the menu for our party. "Don't you think so, Jessica?"

"Mmm hmm." I swallowed a huge bite. "Everything on this table is delicious." I was already feeling a little full, but that wasn't going to stop me from sampling everything. After all, if we wanted our party to be the best, we had to have the best food, and it was my job to sort it all out. I wondered if I could get a job doing this for the rest of my life . . . official taste-tester.

"Daddy discoverd Jean Jacques when he was in Paris," Lila said, referring to the Fowler's newly hired chef. "Isn't he amazing?"

"Jean Jacques," Ellen said with a French accent.

"Wouldn't it be cool to have *two* first names?"

I giggled and dug in to the French garlic bread.

"As far as I'm concerned, we could have all of the stuff on this table for our party," Kimberly declared. "Only we'd need about a hundred times as much."

"I don't know if Daddy would spring for all that," Lila said. "Maybe we can narrow it down to five or six things."

Mandy let out an exaggerated sigh. "Oh, OK. If we *must*."

"Darling, pass the shrimp cocktail," I said, holding out my hand in a dainty way.

"Why, certainly, Lovey!" Mandy replied, handing me the fancy glass dish.

Kimberly dabbed the corners of her mouth with a napkin. "OK. Enough fooling around. We have an important decision to make."

"Yes. We need to pick either the blue or the green linen," Lila said, fingering the tablecloth.

"No, not that," Kimberly said, shaking her head. "We still haven't decided when we're going to have our party. Let's pick a night so we can start inviting people."

Mandy set down her glass of sparkling apple cider. "Well, I was talking to Elizabeth at the Child Care Center this afternoon. She told me when their party is, so I think we ought to pick another night."

Kimberly looked at her eagerly. "And when is their party?"

"Friday," Mandy said. "Seven o'clock, I think."

I looked at Kimberly. Was she thinking the same thing I was?

"Well, then. I guess that settles it," she said, grinning at me.

"Our party will be Friday night, too," I finished, glad that she seemed to be on my wavelength.

"But—" Mandy began to protest.

"Why would we—" Ellen started to say.

"Because," Kimberly said, taking a bite of shrimp, "when everyone decides to come to our party instead of the Angels', it will be absolutely obvious which club is the better club!"

Mandy shifted in her chair. "Do you really think that's a good idea?"

"Yeah. Why not?" Kimberly asked with a shrug.

"I don't know." Mandy moved her miniature egg roll around on her plate. "It just seems like . . . maybe there will be some people who want to go to both, so we might not get all the guests we want."

Lila, Kimberly, and I all stared at her. "Right. Like that's going to happen!" I said.

"I don't think there will actually be much of a choice," Lila said. "Once people hear about our fantastic food and our DJ—"

"The Angels won't stand a chance," Kimberly finished triumphantly.

Mandy sighed. "I don't know. It makes me feel really weird, competing with the Angels like this."

"Why?" Kimberly asked.

"Well, because. I was one once. And I'm still friends with them," Mandy insisted.

"Well, look at me!" I said. "I'm friends with Elizabeth, too. I mean, it doesn't *get* any closer than being twins, right?"

Mandy laughed. "No, I guess it doesn't."

I smiled at her. "And just because Elizabeth and I are twins, does that mean I shouldn't be excited about a Unicorn party, and I shouldn't have a great time on Friday night?"

"Of course not," Mandy said. "I see your point, I guess."

"Then it's settled!" I declared.

"And don't worry about being competitive," Ellen piped up. "This business book I'm reading says it's a natural part of life."

"Thanks, Professor Riteman," Lila told her.

"You're welcome," she replied, licking up some cocktail sauce that was trickling down her chin.

"Anyway, since this is a club party, I have a menu suggestion," Lila said. "How about if we serve *club* sandwiches?"

"Not just club sandwiches—Unicorn Club Sandwiches! That's a great idea!" I cried. Our plan was getting better by the second.

"OK . . . but the only purple ingredient *I* can think of is spoiled meat!" Mandy commented.

Kimberly wrinkled her nose. "Yuck. Maybe we should just have grape punch instead."

When I got home, I dashed upstairs and knocked on Elizabeth's door. "Hey, Elizabeth. Can I come in?" Without waiting for a reply, I opened the door and sauntered into her room. "Hi. I have something kind of important to tell you."

Elizabeth turned around from her desk. "Really? How was your dinner at Lila's?"

"I'm stuffed." I patted my stomach. "It was the best gourmet meal I've ever had. We were tasting different dishes to decide on the menu for our party. Mr. Fowler's going to spring for just about anything we want, can you believe it? It's really going to be the party of the century."

"Not that you've ever been known for exaggerating," Elizabeth teased me.

"Never ever." I grinned. OK, so maybe I do tend to make things sound bigger than they are. But this time, it was *true*. "Anyway, Elizabeth, that's what I wanted to talk to you about. You guys might want to think about canceling your party. I mean, I wouldn't want you to be horribly embarrassed."

"Embarrassed?" Elizabeth repeated. "Why would I be?"

"Because everybody will come to our party and nobody will show up at yours," I said. I hated to make Elizabeth feel bad, but a few moments of pain now were better than the humiliation of an empty backyard Friday night.

"Why would that happen?" Elizabeth looked blank. "Our parties aren't going to be on the same night."

I shrugged. "They are now."

"What?" Her eyes widened. "But I thought you

were planning yours for Saturday, or the next weekend, or—"

"We were," I said. "But we had a change in plans tonight."

"Really? Why?" Elizabeth sounded perplexed.

"The weather's supposed to be nice on Friday. It just seems like a good day for a party," I said casually.

Elizabeth's eyes narrowed. "Right." She closed her textbook with a smack. "Don't even try to act like you picked Friday out of the blue," she said angrily. "I'm sure you found out about our plans, and that's when you changed yours. I don't know how you found out—you must have been eavesdropping at school today, which is totally predictable. I guess one of the requirements for being a Unicorn is having absolutely no morals!"

"We have plenty of molars—I mean, morals," I snapped back. "That's a horrible thing to say!"

"Well, stealing our Friday night is a horrible thing to *do*!" Elizabeth shot back, tossing her pen onto the desk.

"Can we help it if we picked the same night as you?" I cried.

"Yes—you could change it," Elizabeth replied. "But you'd never do that. You're a Unicorn, and being a Unicorn means being nasty and unfair!"

"Is that so?" I could feel my heart pounding. "Well, if it's so horribly *awful* to be a Unicorn, then how come Mandy quit *your* boring, goody-goody club to come back to *ours*?"

Elizabeth's face fell, and she looked like she was

on the verge of tears. Suddenly I felt terrible for saying something so hurtful. "I—I didn't mean that," I said quickly.

"Yes, you did." Elizabeth's voice trembled. She turned around and snapped open her textbook. "I'm trying to study, so would you please go?" She was slumped over her book, her back to me.

My feet wouldn't move. How could she just kick me out, after I'd tried to apologize? I *did* feel bad about what I'd said, but it wasn't like she didn't deserve it. I mean, she did call my friends "nasty and unfair." What Unicorn in her right mind would take that? "Listen, Elizabeth—"

"Now?" Elizabeth spat out the word.

I slowly turned around and walked out the door, my heart beating furiously. The fights between the Angels and the Unicorns in the past were pretty bad, but I had a feeling we hadn't seen anything yet. The real war was about to begin.

I shoved a notebook onto the top shelf of my locker Tuesday morning. Three pens came flying out and onto the floor. I picked them up and tried to put my books inside, but I'd left a couple of sweaters and a sweatshirt in there, and there wasn't enough room. "Agh!" I cried in frustration.

I was in a terrible mood. Even the thought of my date with Todd for Friday night couldn't erase how angry I felt at Jessica. Why did she have to try to ruin the only fun thing the Angels had planned lately? Couldn't the Unicorns just look the other way—for once? I slammed my locker door shut.

"Umm . . . Elizabeth?" Mandy was standing on the other side of my locker. "Rough morning?" she asked quietly, taking a step closer.

"Rough night," I admitted. Looking at Mandy, I couldn't help remembering what Jessica had said the night before. *If it's so horribly awful to be a Unicorn, then how come Mandy quit your boring, goody-goody club to come back to ours?* I pushed the thought out of my mind. Mandy hadn't quit the Angels because she didn't like being an Angel; she wanted to be in both clubs, but she couldn't. So she'd made a tough choice. "How are you?" I asked Mandy, trying to shake my bad mood.

"Not so hot. I, umm, need to apologize for something," Mandy said, staring at the scuffed linoleum floor. "And I feel really awful about it."

"About what?" I asked. I couldn't imagine Mandy doing anything she needed to apologize for.

"Last night, I told the Unicorns that your party was this Friday night," Mandy murmured.

"Oh. So that's how Jessica found out," I said. "I thought she was eavesdropping or something." It was almost a relief to know Jessica hadn't been *quite* that underhanded.

"No, it was me," Mandy said sheepishly. "I know you're probably mad at me, but I only told them because I wanted to make sure our parties wouldn't be on the same night!" She looked at me intently. "That way, we could go to each other's parties. Only Kimberly didn't see it that way."

"I should have known Kimberly was involved,"

I mumbled. Then I cleared my throat. "Sorry—I know she's your friend."

"It's OK. Anyway, as soon as the word 'Friday' was out of my mouth, Kimberly was penciling it in on the calendar—for the Unicorn party!" Mandy sighed. "I tried to talk everyone else out of it, but they wouldn't listen. I'm *really* sorry, Elizabeth. The last thing I wanted was for us to be in this weird competition for best party."

"Really, don't worry about it." I managed a smile. "I mean, it's not great, but . . . it's not your fault, either."

"The thing is, if we had two parties, on two separate nights, it would be a major improvement to the social life around here! It's totally stupid to pack it all into one night." Mandy leaned against the locker next to mine. "I mean, we all know how bad Saturday night TV is—couldn't *one* club have their party then and give us all a break?"

I laughed. "Too bad no one else feels that way."

Mandy nodded as the bell rang. "So what are you going to do now?"

"Go to homeroom?" I said.

"No—about your party, silly." Mandy punched me lightly on the arm. "And I'm not spying, I promise. I'm just curious."

I shut my locker door. "Oh, I don't know. But we'll think of something."

We had to. I wasn't about to let Jessica and the Unicorns get away with sabotaging our party Friday night.

Six

"Now, we're not going to get depressed about this," I told the Angels after school that day. We were sitting on the front steps of the building, planning our next move.

"We're not?" Evie said, kicking a small rock down the steps.

"No, we're not," Mary declared strongly.

"OK then. What *are* we going to do?" Maria sighed, looking at Mary for an answer.

"Well . . ." Mary hesitated. "I don't know yet. But we're not going to sit around feeling bad about it!"

"The whole point of having a party was to make us feel better about our club," I said. "Only now we feel terrible because we have to compete with the Unicorns again."

"Why couldn't they just let us have our party Friday—and have theirs Saturday? I mean, what would be the big deal?" Evie wondered.

"Because the only fun for them in having a party is in ruining ours." Maria shook her head disgustedly.

"Well, maybe we should take a vote," I suggested. I didn't want to give up on the idea of an Angels' party. If we let the Unicorns push us around this time, they'd only do it again—or else gloat about it for the rest of the year. "Who wants to go ahead with our party Friday night and who wants to—"

"Excuse me, but *what* did you just say?"

I whirled around. Kimberly was standing on the step above us, with Jessica and Lila right behind her. She was looking down at the Angels with a sneer. She can be so rude, it's unbelievable. It's like she's been studying all the mean characters in books and movies and memorizing them, so she can act just as horrible.

"Were we talking about canceling our poor little party?" Kimberly asked, her mouth puckered into a fake pout.

I tried to look composed. "No, *we* weren't—"

"Actually, yeah," Evie blurted out at the same time.

"Oh, a difference of opinion." Kimberly smirked and turned to Jessica. "I told you—this is called dissension in the ranks."

"It's not dissension, Kimberly, and we're not—" I started to protest, but just then I saw Todd coming out the front doors of school. My jaw went slack. I knew I was supposed to be telling Kimberly off, but somehow I'd forgotten exactly what I wanted to say. "You know, we're not . . . like . . ."

"You're not *what*?" Kimberly demanded. "Honestly, Elizabeth, you've become a major space cadet. Is that a new club requirement?"

Lila and Jessica snickered.

That did it. My heart was racing from embarrassment and anger—and determination. Seeing Todd reminded me that we *had* to go through with our party Friday night—or I'd have to cancel our one and only date!

I stood up, facing Kimberly. "*As* I was saying before you so *rudely* interrupted me, we're *not* canceling our party, and there's no so-called dissension in the ranks."

The rest of the Angels got up, too, so we were all standing face-to-face with Kimberly, Jessica, and Lila.

"We're friends, so we don't have ranks," Maria said. "We're all equals."

"And Elizabeth's right—our party is definitely still on for Friday night," Mary told them. "So maybe you should be worried about yours."

Jessica laughed. "Why?" she asked, as if the suggestion were ludicrous. "What would we possibly worry about? We already know that everyone who's anyone is planning to be there."

"Are you sure?" I asked, raising one eyebrow. "Because last time I checked, everyone had already been to a million parties at Lila's." I patted my mouth, pretending to yawn. "Why would anyone want to go to boring old Fowler *Crust* again?"

Lila took a step toward me. "Wait a second, nobody says that about—"

Jessica put a hand on Lila's arm, restraining her. "For your information, Elizabeth, the party isn't even *at* Lila's. You're so spacey and out of it, you don't even know that! Come on, you guys, let's get out of here." She, Lila, and Kimberly walked down the steps, holding their heads high.

"What did she mean by that?" Evie wondered, gazing after them.

"I don't know, but we'd better find out," I declared. I didn't know what made me more mad: Kimberly acting so high-and-mighty around me— or Jessica! "And whatever happens . . . we're *not* calling off our party!"

"I don't see what was so bad about having the party at my house," Lila grumbled, handing me a cup to rinse. The two of us were washing dishes at the Child Care Center at the end of the afternoon.

Kimberly was sitting on the window ledge. Volunteering at the Center isn't exactly her favorite thing to do; she usually only comes along so she can hang out with the rest of the Unicorns. "Yeah, Jessica," she said. "We had the whole thing planned, and then just because your sister calls it Fowler Crust, we have to call it off? I suppose she thinks that's funny."

I resisted the urge to giggle. It *was* kind of funny, now that I thought about it. Mr. Fowler is about as upper-crust as a person can get. "Nothing's wrong with your house, Lila. I just couldn't let them get the best of us, so I had to say something!"

Lila sniffed. "*Well*, I *guess* so." She sighed, handing

me a plate. "But it is one of the biggest mansions in town. Where can we possibly have our party that would be better?"

"Not my house," Kimberly said. "My mother wouldn't let us."

"And not my house," I said, rinsing a bit of extra soap off the plate. "That's, like, impossible—ew! Gross!" I cried. The drain on my side of the sink was clogged, and instead of rinsing soap off the plate, I suddenly had a sink full of rising, dirty water! "Agh! Help!" I turned to Lila, but Lila was already halfway across the room, looking at the sink as if it were going to swallow her whole.

Kimberly came over to take a look. "I have three words for this," she said, making a face. "Dis-gust-ing."

"Well, don't just stand there! Do something!" Lila shrieked.

"Me!" I cried. "Why should I fix it?"

"Because it's on your side of the sink!" Lila replied.

"It only got clogged because *you* kept trying to stuff bread crusts down it!" I argued.

"Look, somebody fix it—before it overflows?" Kimberly hopped back up on the window ledge, keeping her feet off the floor.

"Oh, I'll do it," I grumbled. I went out into the hallway to the utility closet. "As if Little Miss Fowler would ever get her hands dirty," I muttered under my breath as I searched through the closet, knocking brooms and dustpans to the floor.

Suddenly I felt a hand on my shoulder. "Is there

a problem, Jessica?" Mrs. Willard asked.

I turned around, wiping my brow. "Is there ever. The sink's turned into a bathtub . . . a really gross bathtub. Actually, more like a fountain."

"Again!" Mrs. Willard frowned, looking extremely exasperated.

"You mean this happens a lot?" I asked. In that case, I was going to start trying even harder to get out of doing the dishes.

"It happened yesterday *and* the day before. Well, maybe this will help." Mrs. Willard grabbed a long-handled plunger from the back of the closet. "Come on, let's go." She sighed.

I walked eagerly back into the playroom's kitchen area with Mrs. Willard. At least I wouldn't have to deal with it all alone now. "See?" I pointed to the full, greenish-colored water in the sink. Bits of bread and cookies were floating in it. Looking at it, I thought I was going to be sick.

Mrs. Willard dropped the plunger into the water, splattering my shirt and face.

"Agh!" I cried, grabbing a paper towel and trying to rub off the slime.

Kimberly snickered. "Darling, green is one of your best colors!"

"It matches your eyes perfectly," Lila agreed, giggling.

"Very funny. But it's not supposed to be *in* my eye!" I grumbled.

"I'm sorry, Jessica," Mrs. Willard said, shaking her head. "I should have told you to stand back.

Now look out everyone." She jammed the plunger over the drain and worked at it for a minute.

I ran into the bathroom to wash my face. I felt as if I'd just been swimming through a swamp.

When I went back into the kitchen, I heard the drain gurgling. Mrs. Willard had the water on full blast. "Looks fine now," she said. "Sorry about your shirt, Jessica."

I glanced down at my splattered white T-shirt. At least it had been white this morning. But I knew Mrs. Willard was very busy; it wasn't her fault the sink wasn't working right. "That's OK, Mrs. Willard. This thing is old, anyway," I said.

"Kind of like this building," Mrs. Willard complained, looking sadly around the kitchen. She pushed a strand of her hair back behind her ear. "The refrigerator's not running right, the microwave won't even defrost an ice cube—everything around here is breaking down lately! And we don't have nearly enough money to fix even half of the problems."

"That's terrible," I said.

"Is there something we can do to help?" Lila asked.

"No. Thanks for the offer, but I think we need a major fund-raising effort." Mrs. Willard sighed. "Honestly, girls, I don't know whether we'll find the money at all."

I looked at Lila, feeling panicky. What if the Child Care Center closed? What would happen to all the kids? What would happen to my little pal Oliver?

"Don't give up," Lila told Mrs. Willard, looking nervously at the sink. "The sink looks fixed now, right? And I'm sure you can find some way to pay for the other things."

"I hope so," Mrs. Willard said softly.

"I hope so, too!" I agreed. "I mean . . . I don't want *all* my shirts to end up looking like this." I pointed to a splotch on my sleeve.

Mrs. Willard laughed. "Neither do I!"

I smiled. I was glad Mrs. Willard could laugh about it, but I was still worried about the Center. We needed to find one of those rich anonymous donors who could give a bunch of money to the Center. Unfortunately for my wardrobe and Mrs. Willard . . . I just didn't know any.

"Sponge," Jessica said, holding out her hand.

I almost laughed. Jessica sounded like a doctor on television, asking the nurse for a sponge during surgery. Then I remembered that Jessica and I were barely speaking to each other.

I handed her the blue sponge. "Sponge," I said, half hoping Jessica would get the joke.

She didn't. Jessica simply wiped off the counter and the kitchen table, then tossed the sponge back to me—right over my head! It landed in the sink, splashing dishwater into my eyes. "Hey!" I cried, wiping a soap bubble off my cheek.

"Sorry," Jessica said breezily. She started rearranging place mats on the table. "So. Is your party still on for Friday night?" she asked.

"Yes," I said. I didn't plan on saying another word to my sister. Whatever I said, the Unicorns would find some way to use it against me and the Angels. I felt like I was in enemy territory—right in my very own house.

"And it's still going to be here?" Jessica went on, obviously irritated by my short answer.

"Uh-huh." I calmly washed a large saucepan, scrubbing at the sticky spots.

"And what kind of events are you having?" Jessica asked. She took a dish towel off the hook on the refrigerator and started drying the plates.

"Oh, I don't know," I said. "A little of this, a little of that."

"Sounds fascinating," Jessica commented. She dried a few more plates, then turned toward me. "And how are things with the love of your life going?"

"Who?" I said, feeling my cheeks turn pink with embarrassment.

"Todd, who else," Jessica said. "Have you made any progress? Have you talked to him lately? Do you know if he's coming to your party?"

I put a fresh squeeze of dish detergent onto the sponge. I knew Jessica and I were supposed to be fighting, but suddenly I really wanted to tell her about my conversation with Todd. It was too exciting not to share with her, when we were used to sharing everything. "Actually, you know what? When I invited him . . . he called it a date!" I told her excitedly.

"Really." Jessica raised one eyebrow. "That's

impressive. But I wonder how he's going to be in two places at once."

"Two places at once? What do you mean?" I looked at her confusedly.

"Well, you guys might have made a date a couple of days ago, but everything's changed now," Jessica declared. "I mean, I can't exactly see Todd passing up the number-one party of the entire year just for some date he could have with you anytime."

I squeezed the sponge so tightly that water ran out all over the counter. "Todd *will* be at my party," I said, wishing I was as confident about it as I sounded.

"We'll see." Jessica hung her dish towel back on the hook and flounced out of the kitchen, leaving me with the rest of the after-dinner mess to clean up.

But all I could do was stare at the tiny calendar hanging above the sink. How dare Jessica suggest that Todd would rather go to her party than mine, when she knew how much I liked him. I grabbed a plate and scrubbed it viciously. One thing was certain. I wasn't about to lose the club war *or* Todd—to my sister or anybody else!

Seven

I stared at my science textbook. I had read the same passage at least ten times, but at the end of the paragraph, all I could see was the same word, over and over again: *Todd.*

What if he really did pass up the Angels' party to go to the Unicorns'? Maybe he didn't really like me the way I like him, even though he'd used the word *date.* Maybe he talks about *every* party he goes to that way.

But I couldn't help thinking of it as a real date. I had pictured it a thousand times. I'd be welcoming people to my house and casually showing everyone where to find food and games and the pool, and then all of a sudden I would turn around and Todd would be at the door. He'd smile at me, take my hand . . .

But that would never happen if Todd was across

town! Wherever the Unicorns' party was going to be—at Lila's, at the beach, in a convenience store, or at the fountain in the park—I didn't care, as long as Todd didn't end up there.

I took one last look at my science book and realized it was hopeless. I picked the cordless phone off my night table and dialed Maria's number. "Hi," I said when she answered. "What's up?"

"Nothing. I'm just sitting here, doodling the word *party* instead of studying." Maria laughed. "Good thing we don't have any tests this week, or we'd all bomb."

"I know," I agreed. "Listen, I was just thinking about our party, too. And I have a feeling that we need to make it a little bigger. I mean, more than just a barbecue in the backyard."

"I was thinking the same thing," Maria said. "I don't want people to think our party's boring . . . and I guess it does sound a little on the ordinary side. Not that you don't have a great house!"

"Yeah. I wish we could have it someplace special," I said. "Maybe we could come up with a concept or a theme or something."

"That's a good idea!" Maria agreed enthusiastically. "High concept—like they say in the movies."

I drummed my fingers against my desk. "Hmm . . . I'm thinking, but all I can think of are low concepts." *And Todd. What would Todd like?*

"Well, maybe we should talk about it at lunch tomorrow," Maria suggested. "Four minds are better than two, right?"

"Right," I replied. "In the meantime, maybe we can get our homework done."

"Yeah, right," Maria grumbled. "I guess I should give it a try. Good night!"

"Bye," I said. I was about to hang up when I heard a click on the line, as if somebody had been on another extension. "Hello?" I said, wondering whether the person was still on the line.

"I'm still here," Maria said.

"Oh—Maria," I said. "Did you hear that click?"

"Yeah—I thought you were hanging up," Maria said. "Why?"

"I wasn't hanging up, but I think someone else was." I frowned. "Someone who probably wants to know all about our plans for the party!"

And of course I knew exactly who. I couldn't believe Jessica would stoop so low as to actually listen in on my phone conversations! Well at least Maria and I hadn't discussed a specific plan. And I wasn't going to discuss anything anytime soon, on the phone—not when the line was being infested by a human bug!

I'd get back at Jessica for this, and for the comment she made about Todd. I didn't know how, but I would.

Even if it took me all night to come up with a way, I was going to get revenge!

"You are not going to believe this, Jessica," Kimberly said when I met her on the front steps outside school Wednesday morning. "I was just about to tell everyone else—I have some amazing news."

"So do I!" I said, joining her, Lila, Mandy, and Ellen by the green metal railing.

"Me first," Kimberly declared.

Big surprise.

"OK, go ahead," I said with a sigh.

"Well, I was thinking, what if we had the party at the beach?" Kimberly looked around at all of us, her eyes lit up with excitement. "Well? Isn't that brilliant?"

Lila wrinkled her nose. "Sure, if you want every beach bum and surfer dude in the state of California at our party."

"Plus how would we carry all the food and stuff down to the beach, and where would we put it?" Ellen asked.

Mandy twisted her lips, looking thoughtful. "Yeah, I see a lot of sand sticking to our cheese and crackers."

"Sorry, Kimberly," I added, "but I don't think so."

Kimberly sniffed. "Well, at least *I* came up with an idea, which is more than I can say for you guys. And it *is* already Wednesday." She folded her arms across her chest and glared off across the lawn.

I cleared my throat. "Well, umm, actually, I was working on our party, too. In a different way." I stepped closer and lowered my voice. "I listened in on a phone call last night between Elizabeth and Maria."

Kimberly snapped her head around and grabbed my arm. "You didn't!" she squealed, sounding thrilled.

Mandy's face darkened. "No, really. Tell me you didn't."

I looked at her pleadingly. "It's the only way. I mean, we can plan our party only if we know what they're planning."

"So what did you find out?" Ellen asked eagerly.

"Well . . . nothing, exactly," I admitted. "But I did find out that they don't know what *they're* doing, either."

"Wait a second—aren't they having a barbecue at your house?" Ellen asked.

"Maybe yes, but maybe no," I said. "They want to make it more special."

"Well, duh." Kimberly shook her head in disbelief. "Who wouldn't?"

I grit my teeth. I was starting to wish we were having the party at Kimberly's, so Lila and I could both sit around and criticize *her* house. Of course, she wouldn't think there was anything wrong with her house, with its five bedrooms, two and a half bathrooms, massive kitchen—

Kitchen. That made me remember something. "Oh, my gosh, you guys. I just remembered—I had the worst dream last night." I shuddered.

"You dreamed that we had a party . . . and nobody came?" Ellen guessed.

"No, of course not!" I said. "I dreamed that I was over at the Child Care Center, and that the sink . . . you know, the one in the kitchen that backed up yesterday? I dreamed that I was trying to use that plunger thing, and I put it over the drain and—ooh!

It pulled me into the sink! I can't tell you how disgusting it was, being sucked down the drain with a bunch of cookie pieces and soggy crackers and—"

Lila held up her hands. "Enough already with the description!"

"Please, I just ate breakfast," Kimberly protested, turning slightly green.

"All I can say is, I was never happier to wake up than I was this morning." I brushed a piece of lint off my black T-shirt. "And I hope Mrs. Willard gets that sink fixed soon, because I don't want to have a dream like that ever again!"

Mandy's face lit up. "Wait a second. Wait a second. Your nightmare just gave me a great idea!"

"Buy some drain cleaner on our way to the Child Care Center today?" Lila asked. "Better make it extra-professional strength."

"No—this is what I'm thinking," Mandy went on excitedly. "See, the Child Care Center needs a whole bunch of things fixed, right? And we need a place to have our party, and we want some kind of special theme or reason for it. So why not *combine* the two, and have a fund-raiser for the Center—at the Center?"

A smile spread across Kimberly's face. "That could work really well."

"It'll definitely make people think we're a good club," Ellen agreed. "Plus I'd love to help Mrs. Willard!"

I was just standing there with my mouth hanging open. Talk about a great idea! No wonder we had wanted Mandy back in the Unicorns so badly!

"This is perfect! We'll be killing two problems with one stone!" I cried.

"That's birds," Lila corrected me. "Kill two birds with one stone."

"Who wants to kill birds?" I said with a wave of my hand. "We have a party to arrange!"

Todd's presence has this way of blocking out everything and everyone else in the cafeteria. Whenever he's around, I can't see anything but him. Wednesday at lunch, I was sitting at the Angeliner, watching him walk over to meet up with his friends. And even though it was incredibly crowded and noisy, I swear I could hear his laugh. It's like . . . Todd radar or something.

"So. Who has a brilliant idea?" Maria looked around the lunch table at all of us.

"My brilliance has been declared . . . *absent* from school today," Evie said, wrinkling her nose. "You should have heard the dumb answer I gave in algebra—and that's my best subject! I usually know everything."

"I think I left my brain in my locker," Mary joked, stirring her yogurt. "Elizabeth, that leaves you."

"Me?" I forced myself to look away from Todd, even though he did look even cuter than the day before. This was more important, at least for the moment. "Well, I don't have any ideas yet. And I'm getting worried, because it's already Wednesday."

"No kidding! If we don't change our plan by tomorrow, we might as well forget about it," Evie complained, mashing the macaroni and cheese on her plate with a fork.

"How about if we go to a party store this afternoon—I bet we'd get some great ideas!" Mary suggested, her face lighting up.

I sighed. "I can't. I promised Mrs. Willard I'd stop by the Child Care Center. She needs some help with . . . well, everything, actually." I knew that the Center was running low on funds and supplies, and that a lot of appliances needed fixing, too. I frowned. *Low on funds*, I repeated to myself. An idea was starting to form in my brain. . . .

Maria looked at me curiously. "What's up, Elizabeth? You've got this really intense expression on your face."

"You're not thinking about who to invite to our party, are you?" Evie teased.

"N-no." I slowly shook my head. "I just figured out what we should do! We'll have the party *at* the Child Care Center—and we'll make it a fundraiser!" I looked eagerly around the table at my friends. "Well?"

"That's perfect," Evie said. "The Center needs money, we need a party—"

Maria grinned. "It's a great idea, but what's the theme going to be?"

I shrugged. "We can figure that out when we go to the Center this afternoon—we can look around and see what would fit."

"Here's what we can do!" Mary said, sitting up in her chair. "We make it a secret theme—you know, a party at our very special and *secret* location!"

I nodded eagerly. "That way the Unicorns won't find out where it is, so they can't ruin it—"

"Plus it adds some mystery, which will make even *more* people want to come," Evie added.

"And that means we'll raise even more money!" Maria declared. "And you know what that will do?" She smirked. "Show everyone that the Angels not only know how to have fun—but we care about other people, too."

"This is perfect," Evie said with a happy sigh. "And what's so perfect is that there's no way the Unicorns can ever compete with this!"

Out of the corner of my eye, I could see Ellen and Kimberly walking past our table at just that second. Ellen paused beside Evie. "Compete with what?"

"Oh. Nothing," Evie said, trying to keep a straight face.

"You weren't talking about your cute little party, were you?" Kimberly gave me a superior smile. "I heard you were having a little trouble thinking of an idea last night. What, can't you decide between the clown or the magic show?" She and Ellen snickered.

I glared at Kimberly. Five minutes ago, that would have upset me. But now we had a new plan, one that Kimberly would never guess. "Actually, we've got it all figured out," I told Kimberly, feeling bold. "And our party is guaranteed to be a major smash, thanks to our new plan."

Kimberly looked at Ellen, rolling her eyes. "Right, Elizabeth."

"For your information, we also have a totally new party idea," Ellen announced in a haughty voice.

"You don't say," Mary grumbled. "How thrilling for you."

"Actually, 'thrilling' *is* the word that comes to mind," Kimberly said with a phony smile. "In fact, it's going to be the event of the year."

"Hmm. We'll see." Maria shot Kimberly a challenging look.

"Yes, we will see," Kimberly replied. "Friday night, everything's going to become incredibly obvious."

I glared right back at her. "It certainly will." Yes, it will be obvious which club is better, which has nicer members, which actually cares about the community. And which one knows how to throw a great party!

"Come on, Ellen, let's go tell the other Unicorns they'd better be scared," Kimberly said, adjusting her mini backpack. "With their new exciting plan, the Angels might actually steal a guest or two from our party—and that would leave us with only two hundred!"

Ellen giggled, and the two of them went over to the Unicorns' table.

Once they were gone, I burst out laughing. "They're so arrogant, it's incredible!"

Maria gazed at them across the cafeteria, shaking her head. "I hope nobody goes to their party."

"They won't, thanks to your great idea," Evie predicted, tapping me on the arm with her straw.

I was so excited about our new party plan, I only stared at Todd once or twice over the rest of lunch period.

That's when I knew it must be a great idea!

Eight

"Do you think she'll say yes, Jessica?" Ellen asked.

"She has to," I declared as we walked down the hall to Mrs. Willard's office. Actually I was so wound up, I was practically skipping. Ever since I'd come up with our party idea that morning, I hadn't been able to think about anything else.

OK, if you want to get all technical about it, maybe Mandy had had the idea . . . but if I hadn't mentioned my sink nightmare, I'm sure the idea would never have crossed her mind.

"Mrs. Willard? Do you have a second?" I asked, knocking lightly on the door. Beside me, Ellen fidgeted with the notebook in her hand.

"I have a second—but that's about it," Mrs. Willard said, looking up from a tall pile of paperwork. She took off her reading glasses. "Come on in."

Ellen and I walked into her office, and I closed the

door behind us. For all I knew, the Angels were volunteering at the Center that afternoon. I wasn't about to let them steal my—er, Mandy's—fabulous idea!

"Mrs. Willard, we have a proposal for you," Ellen said, sitting down. "And as president of the Unicorn Club, it is my pleasure to inform you that we have decided to hold a fund-raiser for the Center."

"You—you have?" Mrs. Willard sat up in her chair, and it creaked loudly. "But—when? How?"

I perched on the edge of a metal folding chair, facing her. "We've got the whole thing figured out. We're going to have a casino night here! Isn't that the most fun thing you've ever heard?"

"Casino night? Gambling?" Mrs. Willard sounded appalled. "With the children here?"

"No, not like that." I giggled. *As if!* "It'll be a Friday night—this Friday night, to be exact. Long after the kids have all gone home. Everyone will buy a bag of chips to gamble with—poker chips, you know, with those cute little colors—for a couple of dollars. But the chips won't be worth anything, so it's not going to be like real gambling."

"And the money we take in from selling the poker chips will go right into the Center's emergency fund, to pay for all the stuff you need to get fixed around here," Ellen continued.

"Like that nasty, disgusting sink problem," I said with a shudder.

A smile slowly spread across Mrs. Willard's face. "That would be nice. I'm not exactly enjoying my second career as a plumber."

"So what do you say?" I asked eagerly, scooting forward. "Can we have it here on Friday night?"

"Friday night . . . that doesn't give you much time," Mrs. Willard said. She shuffled some papers on her desk, uncovering her calendar. "Today's Wednesday . . ."

"Believe me—when we set our minds to something, we don't *need* much time," Ellen declared, interrupting her. "Two days is enough because there are five of us, remember?"

"So what will it be?" I asked eagerly. "Are you going to help us save the Center or not?"

"Well!" Mrs. Willard exclaimed. "If you're going to put it *that* way, Jessica . . . how can I say no?"

Ellen and I exchanged high fives. "All right!" Ellen cried.

"We won't let you down," I promised. "We're going to raise a ton of money. Everyone at school's going to come." Well, almost everyone. Except the few random nerds who show up at Elizabeth's party. "We'll take care of everything. We just need two things from you, Mrs. Willard." I cleared my throat.

Mrs. Willard smiled. "Sounds easy. What would those two things be?"

"One, we need you to be here at the beginning and the end, to unlock the place," I said.

Mrs. Willard nodded. "I think I'll do some work in my office during your party. It never hurts to have an extra adult around, just in case. But I promise, I'll be invisible—unless anyone needs me."

"OK. And two," I continued, "we need you to promise not to say a word to Elizabeth, Maria, Mary, or Evie about this. It's a secret party, and nobody can know what we're planning. *Especially* not the Angels."

Mrs. Willard knit her brow. "But aren't they invited? Won't they find out eventually?"

"Eventually, yes," I said, feeling a little flutter of excitement. They'll know, like, the day *after* the party! "But the thing is . . . they're already planning another party, for the same night."

"Two parties on the same night? Isn't that sort of silly?" Mrs. Willard looked confused.

"No," Ellen said, completely straight-faced. "Actually, it's the only thing to do."

"Didn't you girls give any thought to having one big party together?"

I sighed. Why does everyone keep saying that?

"I mean, even if you aren't in the same clubs anymore, can't you still be friends?" Mrs. Willard continued.

"Maybe," I told her. "But having a party together? That's basically . . . unheard of."

"See, Mrs. Willard, there's a lot you don't know about," Ellen said, standing up. "Frankly, I don't want to go into it right now, but let's just say that the Angels and the Unicorns have a major difference of opinion."

"About?" Mrs. Willard asked.

"Everything," I declared. "So will you promise to keep our casino night a secret?"

Mrs. Willard shrugged. "If you don't want me to say anything, I won't."

"Thanks a million. Now sit back and get ready to count the cash—we have some supplies to rent!" I rushed to the door.

"Don't look now, but there are spies here," I whispered to Ellen, jerking my head toward the aisle marked STREAMERS AND BALLOONS. The unmistakable sound of Elizabeth's laughter floated over toward where we were standing in the "Special Themes" aisle.

"Let's get out of here," Ellen said, sounding panicked.

"Relax." I put my hand on her arm. "Let's get a little closer. We might learn something interesting."

Ellen giggled. "This is so exciting. I feel like I'm on a police show."

We crept down to the end of the aisle. I tried to get a peek at Elizabeth, but the display of feather boas was too tall for me to see over. I stepped up on the small ledge of the display shelf and tried to hide in the midst of the clump of boas. A pink feather tickled my nose.

No, don't do it, I ordered my nose. *Just ignore that ticklish feathery thing and pretend it's not there. You can't—you won't—*

I sneezed. *"Aaachoo!"*

"Jessica? Is that you?"

Sometimes being an identical twin with an identical sneeze is really annoying.

"Oh, uh, *hi*, Elizabeth!" I said cheerfully. I stepped down and went around the corner, where

Elizabeth and Evie were standing. Ellen hovered behind me. "What a coincidence!"

"Really," Elizabeth replied, folding her arms.

"Yeah," I said. I could tell she didn't believe me. "I mean, imagine *you* guys actually having as good an idea as ours."

"Jessica and I have a lot of party supplies to get," Ellen piped up from behind me. "They're kind of . . . special. Like our party."

"Ours too." Elizabeth gave Evie a knowing look. "Well. We have to get going."

"Yeah, we're late," Evie added, and the two of them walked right past me and Ellen, toward the front door.

"But—aren't you going to buy anything?" I called after them.

"We'll come back later." Elizabeth waved goodbye, her lips quivering as if she were trying not to laugh. Then she and Evie ran out the door.

I gazed after them. "What do you think *that* was all about?"

Ellen shrugged. "I don't know, but if they don't buy any supplies, their party's going to be even lamer than we thought!" She giggled.

But I couldn't help feeling suspicious. Something told me my sister was up to something a lot bigger than a barbecue party in our backyard.

"Hi, Mrs. Willard. Thanks for making the time to talk to me and Elizabeth," Evie said, taking a seat in Mrs. Willard's office.

"I'm always here for you," Mrs. Willard responded cheerfully. "That is, when I'm not trying to fix the refrigerator or trying to rescue kids from an overflowing sink." She smiled wryly.

I slid into the chair next to Evie's. "Actually, that's kind of why we're here," I told Mrs. Willard. "We wanted to ask you if we could help."

"Are they teaching electrical repair in middle school now? Wow, things have changed since I was a kid," Mrs. Willard teased.

I grinned. "Not exactly. We don't know how to fix things—not yet, anyway. But we do know how to raise money to pay someone *else* to fix them."

Evie leaned forward in her chair. "This is what we want to do. On Friday night, we—that's us and the other Angels—wanted to have like a mini carnival in the backyard here. We'll charge a little bit for each event, or maybe just charge an admission price. And all the money we make, we'll donate to the Child Care Center!"

Mrs. Willard stared at Evie, and then turned to me. She seemed completely stunned.

"I know it's really last minute," I said. "But I promise, we won't be any trouble at all. I mean, we'll pay for everything—food, soda, decorations—and we've already arranged to borrow the carnival booths and games from school. We'll clean up afterward—"

"You won't even know we were here!" Evie interjected. "Except of course that you'll have some extra money to use to get this place back into shape."

"So what do you say, Mrs. Willard?" I asked. "Can we?"

"Can you?" Mrs. Willard repeated, a smile slowly spreading across her face. "Can you ever! That sounds like a wonderful idea."

"Great!" Evie exclaimed.

"Oh, thank you, thank you, thank you!" I cried.

I started to stand up, when Evie lay a hand on my arm. "There is, umm, one other thing," she said softly, raising an eyebrow at me.

Suddenly I remembered. I let out a short, nervous laugh. "Right. Uh, Mrs. Willard, can you please not tell the Unicorns about our party?"

Mrs. Willard's eyes widened. "Why not?"

I shifted uncomfortably in my seat. I didn't want to bother Mrs. Willard with the details of our war with the Unicorns, but I knew I had to tell her something. "See, they're having their own party the same night, and, well, it's just kind of gotten to this point where we're not exactly sharing our . . . entertainment plans. So we'd really appreciate it if you didn't say anything about this in the next few days."

"Hmm." She tapped her pencil against the calendar on her desk, looking as if she was trying to figure something out. "Well, all right. Though why you two clubs want to have separate parties when you have a lot of the same friends is beyond me."

I sighed as Evie and I stood up to leave. "Trust us," I told her. "This is the only way."

Nine

"Now, the key to this whole thing is, we can't tell anyone what we're planning." I took a sip of my milk shake. It was an hour later, and Evie and I met up with the other Angels at Casey's ice cream parlor, one of our favorite hangouts at the mall. "Not where it is, or what it is, or anything."

"Who am I going to tell?" Maria said with a shrug. "You guys are my best friends."

"I might confide in my cat, but that's it," Evie promised. She leaned back in the booth seat, picking up her dish of strawberry ice cream. "And she won't meow a word to anybody."

Mary licked a glob of hot fudge off her spoon. "There's only one problem."

"What's that?" I asked.

"Well, it's easy for *us* to stay away from the Unicorns," she said, gesturing toward Maria and

Evie. "But you *live* with one. How are you going to keep this a secret from Jessica?"

"Easy. We keep secrets from each other all the time," I assured her, though privately I saw her point. It wasn't easy keeping secrets from my twin. We usually tell each other everything. But this time, I was determined to keep my mouth shut.

"Yeah, but remember how she tried to listen in on our phone conversation last night?" Maria said. "She might do some more spying."

"You're probably right," I agreed, tapping my spoon against my glass. "Well . . . it's kind of the supreme sacrifice, but . . . I guess I just won't be able to talk to you guys on the phone for the next few days."

"No!" Maria gasped. "Anything but that!" She giggled.

"Maybe we can come up with some kind of code words," Evie suggested. "Like in spy movies. You know, when somebody calls and all they say is, 'the eagle flies at midnight!' "

I laughed. I could just imagine Jessica trying to figure out that one.

I was thinking up some more code words we could use when there was a loud greeting across the ice cream parlor. "Yo, Wilkins!"

I looked over toward the door and saw Todd walking into Casey's. He waved to acknowledge his friends, then, before sitting down with them, quickly glanced around the restaurant.

I felt my face turn pink. *Don't get embarrassed*, I

told myself, trying to calm down. *There's nothing to be embarrassed about.* I wiped my mouth with a napkin. *At least not yet.*

Todd sat down without seeing me. I didn't know whether to feel relieved or disappointed.

"You know, something tells me that Jessica will do everything she can to find out about our party," Mary predicted. "She's a pretty major snoop. I mean, even you have to admit, Elizabeth, that she's gone to some pretty incredible lengths in the past just to make trouble."

I pried my eyes from Todd and looked at Mary. Something had suddenly clicked into place. Jessica *would* go out of her way to ruin our party. And she knew that I like Todd and that I'd invited him to my party. If she wanted to get information about the party, she'd probably go straight to him! She *might* even go so far as to pretend to be *me*. It wouldn't be the first time.

"You know what?" I said. "I think there's a way we can out-spy Jessica."

"How?" Maria asked.

"I think they call it . . . counterintelligence," I said deviously.

"That doesn't sound good," Evie commented. "Doesn't that mean stupidity?"

"No." I laughed. "It means . . . giving bad information to a spy because you know she's *going* to spy. So she thinks she knows the truth—but she doesn't!"

Mary grinned. "I like the sound of that."

Now all I had to do was get up my nerve to go

through with it. I took a deep breath. Anything for the Angels!

I watched as Todd tossed his napkin onto the table and picked up his blue denim jacket. That was my cue.

I stood up. "I'll be right back," I told everyone at the table.

"Good luck," Evie said, crossing her fingers.

I tried to ignore the knot in my stomach as I approached Todd. We hadn't really talked much since the day I'd invited him to the party. As I got closer, I felt even more nervous. It would have helped if he didn't look totally cute today. As if he ever *wasn't* totally cute.

Todd was already walking out of the mall by the time I caught up to him.

"Hi!" Todd said. "Where did you come from?"

"I was in Casey's—I saw you leave," I explained. "And . . . see, I need to talk to you about something."

"Really?" Todd asked. He looked concerned. "Is it about Friday night?"

"Kind of," I said.

"You're not going to . . . break our date or something, are you?" Todd asked, scuffing his sneaker against the sidewalk.

"No!" I felt a surge of nervousness and excitement. He was still calling it a *date.* And he actually sounded concerned that I was going to break it. As if I ever would! "It's nothing to do with our . . . date." I cleared my throat. "It's that I need to ask you a favor."

"Want me to bring something?" Todd asked. "Help invite people?"

"No . . . actually, I want you to make sure that some people *don't* come to our party," I said.

Todd frowned. "That doesn't sound like you."

"Oh—not like that!" I said. "I mean, of course everyone's welcome. Everyone except . . . the Unicorns, that is. See, they're having their own party on the same night. And they're determined to ruin ours."

Todd's face relaxed a little. "So what does that have to do with me?"

"Well, you know how Jessica is," I said. "She'd do anything to get the best of us. Including lying, cheating, spying—"

"You sure love your sister, don't you?" Todd joked.

I smiled. "Of course. It's just that when it comes to our clubs, things can get a little ugly."

Todd nodded. "Uh-huh. OK. So what can I do to help? You want me to handcuff Jessica? Keep her under surveillance for the next few days?" He grinned.

"Not exactly." I smiled back. "But close. I have an idea of what she might try. And here's what I want you to do."

"OK. Let me run down the checklist we've got so far," Kimberly announced on Wednesday afternoon. "Mr. Fowler's rented the blackjack table, the roulette table, the poker table—"

"Does anyone actually know how to *play* all these games?" Lila interrupted.

"I know how to play—I'll teach you guys," Mandy offered. "I learned a lot of card games when I was in the hospital. We used to bet with straws."

Mandy had been sick with cancer a year ago. I still couldn't believe how strong she'd been through the whole thing. Fortunately, now she is a hundred percent healthy.

"And were you a good player?" Ellen asked.

Mandy rested her arm on the back of the couch in Kimberly's living room. "Darling, I was the best. They called me Poker-Face Miller."

"OK, so Mandy's our resident gambling expert." Kimberly made a note on a piece of paper. "Lila, you and your dad are taking care of all the casino supplies, like cards, chips, roulette wheel, et cetera."

I stared out the window. Planning parties is boring compared to having the party itself. Everyone could talk about the casino night all they wanted, but until it actually happened, I was more interested in finding out what the Angels were up to. I couldn't forget how Elizabeth and Evie had acted in the party store that afternoon—like they were pulling something on us. Who did they think they were, even trying to compete with the Unicorns? Nobody could come up with a better idea than us . . . could they?

"Ellen, I'm putting you in charge of making a map to the Child Care Center," Kimberly said.

Ellen wrinkled her nose. "But—I can't draw very well."

Kimberly heaved an enormous sigh. "Oh. All right, *I'll* do the map then. You can take care of getting a money box. All we need are some ones, so we can make change, and something to put all the money in to keep it safe."

"That leaves one very important detail," Kimberly said. "Food!"

Lila sighed. "Too bad Daddy decided that renting all the games *and* hiring Jean Jacques to prepare all that yummy gourmet stuff was a little too much. If you ask me, no amount of luxury is too much." She shook her head. "Honestly, I don't know what gets into Daddy's head sometimes."

"Anyway, Jessica's not doing anything yet," Kimberly said. "She can bring snacks, and I'll bring the soda. OK, Jessica?"

"Oh, sure," I agreed. Whatever. These little party details were so annoying. If you ask me, what we really needed to focus on was spying on Elizabeth and the Angels. Besides, I'd helped come up with the whole idea for the party—wasn't that *more* than enough?

"OK, now let's talk about more important things. What boys are we inviting?" Kimberly asked with a grin.

"Well, I personally am asking Peter DeHaven," Mandy said. "But I bet he'll come only if Aaron comes, so Jessica, make sure you invite him, OK?"

"Oh, yeah, sure. Whatever," I said. And then all of a sudden, the idea hit me. I knew what I could do to find out about the Angels' party. And it was brilliant, absolutely brilliant. "You guys!" I cried. "I have a plan!"

Kimberly cleared her throat. "Jessica, we already

have our plan, in case you haven't been listening."

"Yeah, hel-*lo*." Lila rolled her eyes. "Do the words *casino night* mean anything to you?"

"Not that kind of plan!" I stood up and started pacing. "Elizabeth's in love with Todd Wilkins, right? And—"

"She is?" Mandy interrupted.

"Oh, yeah." I smiled slyly. "Big time. So *anyway*, she's invited Todd to her party."

"And?" Lila asked, looking irritated. "What does that have to do with anything?"

"Yeah. If we have one less person at our party, it won't make a difference," Ellen said. "Even though Todd *would* add to the scenery cuteness factor."

"It's not that Todd won't be at our party," I clarified, getting frustrated. Did everyone have to interrupt every single second? "It's that he'll be at the Angels' party. And if he's going to *be* there, then he'll have to know *where* it is, won't he?"

"Umm . . . *yeah*," Mandy agreed. "Unless he wants to be incredibly late!"

"So it's simple!" I declared. "All I have to do is ask Todd where their secret party is."

"Jessica? I think you're forgetting something." Mandy waved her hand in front of my face as if she were trying to wake me out of a hypnotic trance. "Todd is friends with Elizabeth. So why would he tell *you* about the Angels' party?"

"But that's what's so awesome" I cried. "He's not going to tell *me*." I looked around the living room at everyone and smiled mischievously. Didn't they get it already? "He's going to tell *Elizabeth*—when I fool him into thinking that I'm her!"

Kimberly's eyes shined with excitement. She hopped off the couch and slapped me a high five. "From one schemer to another . . . may I say I respect your talent enormously!"

"What can I say." I shrugged. "I mean, what's the point of being an identical twin if you can't take advantage of it now and then?"

Ten

Sorry, Elizabeth. This probably isn't fair.

But life isn't fair, is it?

I stepped out of the bathroom stall at school Thursday morning, wearing a pale pink cardigan sweater I'd taken from Elizabeth's closet a few weeks ago. I walked up to the mirror, rubbed my Very Berry Pink lip gloss off my lips with a tissue, then pinned my hair back with two identical silver barrettes.

Well, here goes nothing, I thought, walking out into the hallway. I knew Elizabeth had gym third period, so there was no way I'd bump into her. Still, it couldn't hurt to keep a low profile. I walked down the hall quickly, keeping my eyes averted.

"Good morning, Elizabeth!" Mr. Clark, our school principal, said cheerfully as I passed him.

"Hi, Mr. Clark!" I replied. I couldn't help noticing that he sounded a lot more excited to see Elizabeth than he usually was to see me. Of course, Elizabeth knows Mr. Clark from interviewing him for the school newspaper. *I* know him from getting into trouble.

I rounded a corner and spotted Todd up ahead, standing by his locker. There was no time to waste.

I paused for just a second, composing myself—just like all the great actresses do when they want to "get into character." (I'd read about it in *Movie Madness* magazine.)

Then, assuming my Elizabeth walk, I approached Todd. So much was riding on this, and I couldn't blow it—or Elizabeth would find out I'd been spying, and *that* would ruin everything.

"Umm, Todd?" I said, pretending to be shy.

"Oh, hi, Elizabeth." Todd put his books on the top shelf of his locker. "What's up?"

I smiled sweetly. "I just wanted to make sure . . . you're still coming tomorrow night, right?"

"Of course," Todd said. He stared into my eyes as if he were trying to read my true feelings for him. I tried to send him some Elizabeth I-have-a-crush-on-you mind waves.

Todd's eyes are this nice rich, dark brown that I'd never noticed before. Of course, why would I notice a slightly boring and dweeby guy's eyes? Cute eyes didn't make up for a pathetic personality.

"So, I'll see you . . . tomorrow night?" I tried to sound hopeful and innocent, the way Elizabeth would.

"Seven o'clock at your house, isn't that what you said?" Todd asked. "Burgers, hot dogs, Frisbee, softball—"

I nodded eagerly.

"I'll be there," Todd promised.

"Ultrafantastic!" I cried.

"Ultrawhat?" Todd seemed a bit put off.

I cleared my throat. I guess Elizabeth doesn't really talk like that. "I mean, gee, I'm really looking forward to it and all," I said bashfully.

"Me too." Todd leaned closer, as if he wanted to whisper something in my ear.

What was he doing? Was he going to kiss me on the cheek or something—right in the middle of the hallway?

"I know the location's supposed to be secret," Todd whispered, his breath warm on my ear. "Don't worry. I won't tell anyone. Especially not Jessica."

I smiled. That was what he thought! I let out a little giggle. "OK, well, I should go study. So will you save me a dance tomorrow?"

"I'll save you all the dances," Todd said.

Since when was Todd Mr. Romance? I wondered. I thought he was someone who'd rather stand around trying to catch popcorn in his mouth than dance with a girl.

I touched the barrettes in my hair. "Well, see you then. Oh, and thanks for keeping everything secret. You know, you can't trust Jessica at all."

"Oh, I know." Todd shook his head. "OK, see you!"

I turned and walked back down the hall, smiling to myself. There's nothing like completing a successful spy mission. But I had to admit, it was kind of disappointing that Elizabeth hadn't been able to come up with anything more interesting than that silly barbecue idea. What was the point of being a creative writer when you couldn't be creative about anything else?

Well, at least Todd was trying to be loyal to Elizabeth by not giving away the location of the Angels' party. Trying, but not succeeding, I thought happily as I slipped into the bathroom to change back into my own clothes.

"Psst! Elizabeth!"

I had just sat down in English class and was getting my notebook out of my backpack. I looked up to see Maria place a small folded piece of paper on my desk.

"What's this?" I slowly unfolded it. I didn't recognize the handwriting at first.

"Dear Elizabeth," the note said. *"Operation Fool Jessica and the Unicorns went according to plan."*

I smiled. It was from Todd! I continued reading.

"I told her the party's still at your house. She bought it completely! —Todd. P.S. See you tomorrow night!"

I felt myself start to blush. It sounded as if Todd was looking forward to our date as much as I was!

I turned and looked at Todd, who was sitting on the other side of the room. "Thanks!" I mouthed, smiling at him.

"No problem," he mouthed back, grinning.

I couldn't wait to tell the rest of the Angels that we didn't have a thing to worry about now!

*   *   *

"So she thinks it's still at your house?" Evie giggled. It was lunchtime on Thursday, and I was sitting with the rest of the Angels at the Angeliner.

"How did Todd keep a straight face?" Mary asked.

I shrugged. "I don't know. I wish I could have seen her!" I could hardly imagine Jessica trying to imitate me. From what Todd had told me after English class, the whole thing sounded pretty hilarious. And now I knew where my pink sweater had gone!

"Look out. Spy alert," Maria whispered. "Here she comes."

"This should be good." I smirked. "Just follow my lead, everyone."

"Greetings, Angels!" Jessica said breezily, stopping at their table. "How's lunch?" She glanced at everyone's plates. "Oh. Gee. I'm surprised you're having the cheeseburger, Elizabeth."

"Why's that?" I asked, trying not to smile.

"Well. You wouldn't want to get sick of burgers. Besides, too much red meat isn't really good for you." Jessica gave me her phony concerned look.

"It's only one cheeseburger," Evie said with a shrug. "It won't kill her."

"Well, yeah, it's only one now," Jessica replied with a knowing look. "But then tomorrow night at your big cookout, you'll probably have another—"

"Wait a second," I said. "How do you know what I'm doing tomorrow night?" I set my fork down with a clatter.

"Let's just say . . . I have my sources." Jessica wiggled her eyebrows. "And my sources are correct, I guess, because you guys all look totally mortified! Yes, it's true, I know all about your so-called secret location." She twirled her hair, looking very satisfied with herself. "Turns out you guys never changed your plan at all. You just wanted us to think that you had. Well, we're not fooled one little bit."

"Oh, and I suppose listening in on my phone conversations wasn't enough!" I exclaimed. "You had to follow me around town and eavesdrop on me at the Child Care Center and then at the party store and—I suppose you bugged my locker, too!"

Jessica smiled at me sweetly. "Don't have a cow, Elizabeth. After all, it's just one party. You guys can always have another. Like maybe in the *eighth* grade. By that time, everyone will probably have forgotten just how lame your last party was." Jessica flashed one last triumphant smile. Then she turned abruptly and walked away from the table, her nose in the air.

I looked at my friends, holding my hand over my mouth until Jessica was a safe distance away.

"OK . . . one . . . two . . . three!" Maria said, and we all burst out laughing.

"That was beautiful!" Evie gasped between giggles. "She'll never suspect a thing."

"Jessica thinks she has us all figured out," I said. "Boy, is she in for a surprise!"

Eleven

"How does that look?" I asked, standing on the radiator in the front hallway at school Friday morning before the first bell.

"A little higher on the right," Kimberly advised.

"A little lower on the left," Lila piped in.

I tried to adjust the sign we'd made to advertise our party that night. But the sheet of paper we used was so wide, I could barely hold up both corners at the same time. It felt like my arms were about to fall off.

"No—lower," Kimberly said.

"Higher," Lila added when I moved it again.

"A little higher . . . no, lower," Kimberly said.

"Will you guys make up your minds!" I shrieked. "Or someone else can get up here and break their back trying to hold this stupid thing up! Since when am I in charge of sign hanging, anyway?"

"All right, all right," Kimberly grumbled. "Chill, Jessica. It looks fine the way it is." She handed me a long piece of masking tape.

Lila sighed happily. "Tonight's going to be such a blast. All thanks to you, Jessica."

I fastened the sign with another piece of tape and hopped off the radiator. "I did do well, didn't I?"

"Finding out that the Angels still plan to have their party at your house is a major coup," Kimberly said. "It makes it that much easier to convince everyone our party's going to be way more exciting."

"We don't have a thing to worry about," Lila declared. "Especially not when people see this."

I stepped back to admire the sign, which was just a *little* bit crooked.

Special Surprise Party Tonight!!!
Brought to You by
* * * The Unicorn Club * * *

Pick Up Special Secret Instructions
at Casey's Ice Cream Parlor
7 P.M.–10 P.M.
Don't Be Late!
Don't Miss the Party of the Year!

"If anyone looks at this and decides to go to the Angels' party instead, I'll stop wearing these loafers," Kimberly said, pointing to her feet. She'd gotten some high-heeled, chunky brown loafers a few months ago, and she'd hardly taken them off since.

"And I'll . . . start shopping at Big Bob's Bargain Buy-O-Rama!" Lila announced with a giggle.

"Oh, yeah? Well, *I'll* quit being a Unicorn—and join the Angels!" I declared, laughing.

Lila and Kimberly both stopped laughing and stared at me. "You're *not* serious," Kimberly said.

"You wouldn't, Jessica. Tell me you wouldn't," Lila demanded.

"You guys! As if this is some bet I'm worried about losing!" I cried.

Just then the front door opened and students started trickling into the hallway. I smiled as Aaron Dallas walked toward me. Aaron and I have been on a bunch of dates, but we're not really boyfriend-girlfriend. He stopped to look at the sign. "Wow, so this is your big party," he commented.

"Yeah—can you come?" I asked eagerly.

Aaron ran his hand through his short brown hair. "Definitely. Casey's at seven. Sounds cool." He smiled at me and moved on down the hall.

Todd came in with Ken Matthews, right behind Aaron. "Hey, Jessica. What's up?"

I gestured to the sign. "You guys can make it, right?"

"Sure," Ken said with a shrug. "Hey, see you guys tonight—I have to go finish my science homework real quick." He jogged off down the hall.

Todd gazed at the sign, tapping his finger to his chin. "Seven o'clock. I don't know. I might have something else to go to."

"Oh, really?" I giggled. "Is that so?"

Todd looked confused. "Yeah. Elizabeth's having a party and—"

"And I know where it is!" I just couldn't keep it in. "Thanks to you! You know, you and Elizabeth really need to spend more time together, if you're still having trouble keeping us apart."

Todd gasped. "You mean, that—that was *you* yesterday?"

I just grinned at him. "Almost worthy of an Academy Award, wouldn't you say?"

"So . . . wait a minute. Her party's still at your house, right?"

"Far as I know," I replied. "Then again, I *do* get all my information from you." Behind me, I could hear Kimberly and Lila snickering. "Of course, if you want to really have fun tonight, you could drop by our party. Maybe you should reconsider."

"Gee, I'll . . . I'll have to," Todd sputtered. "S-see you later, Jessica. Oh, and please don't tell Elizabeth that I told you about—oh, never mind, the damage is done!" He hurried away, looking very upset.

I put my hand over my mouth. *Sorry, Elizabeth! But Todd's right—what's done is done!*

I stood in the front hallway, staring up at the Unicorns' sign. "It's amazing how complicated this has gotten," I said, unrolling the large sheet of bright red poster board I was carrying. Both clubs had secret locations and special instructions on how to get there. I hoped people wouldn't get confused!

Maria got up onto the radiator, and I climbed up

after her. "You guys tell us if this is straight, OK?" Maria asked Evie and Mary. She and I each took a side of the sign.

"That looks perfect," Evie said after we unrolled the sign. "Even better, it looks *bigger* than theirs!"

"And it's red, which is a natural attention-getter," Mary added.

I laughed as I taped the corners to the wall. Then I hopped off the radiator and stood back to check out our work.

Don't Miss It!
The Party You've Been Waiting for Is . . . Tonight!
Pick Up Your Map at Guido's Pizza Palace
Then Find Your Way
to the Best Party Ever!
See You There!

The Angels

"Add a couple of exclamation marks after the 'See you there,'" I advised Maria, who was holding a large black Magic Marker.

"Do you think we should give any hints?" Mary asked.

I shrugged. "We don't want to give it away."

"Yeah." Maria smiled mischievously. "The more secretive the better."

"So, Elizabeth," Winston Egbert said, walking up to me, "What's all this *secrecy* about?" My friends had all gone to homeroom, but I'd stayed in the hall a little longer, checking out our handiwork.

"It's just something we wanted to do, you know, to make the whole thing more fun." I smiled at him.

"So I don't have to worry about getting into some high-tech espionage?" Winston asked. "Or blowing your cover, or not knowing the code word, or—"

I laughed. "I don't think so. The only thing you have to worry about is getting there. And I'm sure you can do that!"

Winston gazed up at both signs. "'Best Party Ever' versus 'Party of the Year.' Hmm. This is going to be a tough call."

"It's no contest, really," Todd said, coming up behind Winston. He smiled at me.

"Well, it sure *looks* like a contest. May the best club win!" Winston proclaimed, throwing his fist into the air. Then he disappeared into the growing crowd of students heading for homeroom.

I looked at Todd. "I wish he hadn't said that."

"Why?" Todd asked, coming closer to me.

I sighed. "Because. There's just so much pressure. I mean, I don't really think that whoever gets more people at their party is the best club. But we'll be completely bummed out if more people end up at the Unicorns' party."

"Maybe this will make you feel better," Todd said. "Jessica is completely fooled—she doesn't think you have anything special planned. And when everyone finds out what your party really is, they're bound to choose yours over some regular old dancing, potato-chip-eating night."

I giggled. Todd made the whole competition thing sound like fun. "You think so?"

Todd nodded. "Your party's going to be great. Stop worrying, OK?" He reached out and squeezed my hand.

"Oh, I will," I said, my heart pounding. At that moment, I didn't care if Todd was the only one who showed up at our party.

In fact, I was starting to think it might be better that way!

Twelve

"OK, that should about do it!" Mr. Fowler closed the trunk door and brushed some dust off his black double-breasted designer suit. "Everyone into the limo!"

I scrambled to get the seat facing the small television. Whenever I get the chance to ride in Lila's limousine, I want to make the most of it. The way I look at it, I'm just practicing for the day when I have my very own limo.

"We look like a bunch of waiters," Mandy joked, sliding onto the seat next to me. "Or is that penguins?"

"We look better than that!" I protested, fingering the black vest I was wearing over a white blouse. Mr. Fowler had rented the casino-style outfits from the same company he'd gotten all the casino games.

"Yeah, I think we look sharp. And besides, I seriously *doubt* that the Angels have cool coordinating outfits." Kimberly slid onto the seat facing me and crossed her legs. "They're probably standing around now with T-shirts on—"

"And barbecue sauce on their T-shirts," Lila added, closing the door firmly.

"Everyone all right back there?" Charles, the Fowlers' chauffeur, asked through the intercom.

"We're ready!" Ellen cried. "Ready to party, that is." She giggled. "Do we have everything?"

"The trunk's stuffed full, so if you don't have everything, I'll be very surprised!" Mr. Fowler joked. "I think you girls have enough supplies to start your own casino!"

Mandy's eyes brightened. "I can you see it now. 'Mom, I'm dropping out of school. The Unicorns are starting their own casino.'"

I laughed, but I *did* have this vague feeling that I'd forgotten to bring something. I quickly checked my backpack on the floor. I had my house keys, my lip gloss, and my wallet—everything I needed. Well, I was probably just nervous about our party. "Thanks for everything, Mr. F!" I called out the window.

"Yeah. Thanks a million, Daddy," Lila said.

"You're welcome," Mr. Fowler said, leaning through the window. "Now remember, Lila, don't bet the house on anything."

"Don't worry—I won't," Lila replied. "But maybe the limo!"

Mr. Fowler grinned. "Well, you girls have fun!" He tapped the top of the car, signaling to Charles that it was OK to go.

As the long, white car made its way down the curving driveway, Kimberly leaned back in her seat and put her hands behind her head. "This is the life."

"Yeah. I could get used to this," I agreed with a luxurious sigh.

Lila gave me a sideways look. "What are you saying? You *are* used to this. You make me pick you up whenever we go anywhere!"

"Is it my fault my bike's had a flat tire . . . for two years?" I joked.

"Well, all I can say is, I bet the Angels aren't showing up at their party in a limo. A little red wagon, maybe." Kimberly giggled. "Can you imagine? They think *they* have something special planned. You saw the sign! Everyone's going to be really psyched when they go all the way to Guido's—just to find out they should go back across town to your house!" she told me. "For what? A hamburger, a Coke, and a game of croquet? *Please.*"

I grit my teeth. "You know, a party at my house isn't *that* horrible."

"Sure, not if we were there. But consider the guests!" Kimberly made a face. "Not to mention the hosts."

I shrugged and stared out the window. I was getting a little tired of Kimberly criticizing Elizabeth. As far as I was concerned, no one should be allowed to make fun of my sister but me—even if she was an Angel.

"I bet Elizabeth will have a great time," Mandy whispered to me. When I turned to look at her, she smiled. "I mean, she *is* your identical twin—she has to have that same 'life of the party' gene you do, right?"

I giggled. "Right."

"I thought you could put all your things in the big playroom," Mrs. Willard said.

I practically dropped the large, heavy box I was carrying onto the kitchen counter. Inside were decks of cards, bags of poker chips, a roulette wheel, and other supplies. Charles, the chauffeur, was wheeling the slot machine in on a dolly, while Mandy and Ellen carried more boxes.

"This is going to be great," Kimberly said, setting down a bag of decorations she'd brought. "But we're going to have to hurry to get this place into shape by seven!"

"No problem," Lila said, setting down her portable CD player and stack of compact discs. "That gives us . . . oh, no, that only gives us an hour!" She rushed to the decorations bag and started yanking things out, tossing streamers and signs onto the floor.

Mrs. Willard cleared her throat. "Now before you all get busy, I need to tell you something," she said gravely.

I looked up at her. Whatever it was, it sounded serious.

"What is it?" I asked.

Ellen furrowed her brow. "Are you OK? Are the kids OK? Is the building OK?"

"Yes, yes, and yes," Mrs. Willard said. "Sorry—I

didn't mean to scare you. But there is a situation you should know about. Now, because of your generous offer to hold this fund-raiser, I took the liberty of getting some repair work started this afternoon. Unfortunately, what that means is that the backyard is completely dug up. They're working on the pipes back there, and I'm telling you, it's a *mess*."

"So . . . no outdoor dancing under the stars kind of thing?" Mandy asked.

"Not unless you enjoy mud in your shoes—no," Mrs. Willard joked.

"I don't know. Dancing in the mud could be very romantic," I mused. "I mean, if you're a *slug*."

"All joking aside," Mrs. Willard continued, "I have to issue you girls a very strong warning. It's not safe out there, so *please* promise me you won't go into the backyard, and promise me you'll keep your guests away, too."

"Sure," Lila said. "That'll be easy. We can use the kids' crayons over there and make a sign."

"And if people want to dance under the stars? There's always the front yard," Ellen said.

"Anyway, it's not *that* kind of party," Kimberly pointed out.

I shot her a look. Wasn't every party *that* kind of party? "Casinos have dancing, don't they? I mean, people go to Las Vegas to get married, so they must have dancing."

"Yeah. And they also have a bunch of Elvis impersonators, but does that mean we want Elvis at our party?" Kimberly said snootily.

"I'm not sure if anyone remembered to invite him," Mandy mused. "Elvis! Hey, Elvis!" she called, looking up at the ceiling and cupping her hands around her mouth.

I pushed her playfully. "Anyway, you guys," I said, trying to be serious, "we'll have the games over here"—I indicated one side of the room—"and the dance floor right here! People can't gamble *all* night."

Lila raised an eyebrow at me. "You really *haven't* been to Las Vegas, have you?"

"Mrs. Wallace, thank you so much for helping us with all this junk," I told Mary's mother, pulling a board with the words RINGTOSS printed on it out of the back of the van.

"You're welcome, Elizabeth. If I'd known how much stuff it was . . ." Mrs. Wallace made a mock-frazzled face. "No, I'm just kidding. I'm happy to help."

I carried the ringtoss game from the back parking lot into the yard behind the Child Care Center. I passed Evie, who was blowing up balloons for the darts game. Mary was balancing the Test Your Strength! game, and Maria was setting up the fortune-teller's booth.

I glanced at my watch. Everything was going according to plan. In only half an hour, everyone—including Todd—would start showing up.

"Wow. This looks like fun!"

I turned around to see Mrs. Willard walking

toward us. "Hi! Thanks again for letting us use the backyard."

"Oh, I'm glad to do it. Actually, you don't know how glad. I might be getting ahead of myself, but I went ahead and started having some work done here, today, in fact," Mrs. Willard told us.

"Really? Because of us?" Evie asked. "That's great!"

"It is great, but it's also a bit inconvenient," Mrs. Willard said. "I hope it won't affect your plans too much, but I'm afraid I have to ask you to not go inside—except to use the bathrooms by the back stairs, of course. I'm having some electrical work done in the playroom, and they took the ceiling tiles down and there are wires everywhere."

"Don't worry—I won't touch any live wires!" Maria said. "I like my hair the way it is!"

I laughed. "Anyone want a perm?"

"It's not that—in fact, I'm sure the electricians left it safe. But I just don't want to take any chances on, oh, getting wires tangled," Mrs. Willard said. "So will you promise me you'll stay back here?"

"With any luck, we'll be too busy to even think about going anywhere else," Mary told her.

"That's the spirit." Mrs. Willard smiled. "Good luck. I'll come out to test my strength later . . . maybe after dinner!"

She walked away, and I looked at my friends. "We're really going to do this, aren't we?"

"We have to," Mary replied. "Everyone's going to pick up their directions in about ten minutes!"

"I wonder what the Unicorns are doing now?" Evie mused.

"And I wonder where their party is!" Maria added.

"Me too," I said. I felt kind of funny being at a separate party from Jessica. I couldn't remember ever hosting a party without my sister there beside me. Even if things had been kind of strained between us lately, I hoped Jessica would have fun tonight.

But I also couldn't help hoping that the Angels' party was a bigger smash than the Unicorns'!

"It's seven-fifteen. Where *is* everybody?" Lila complained, looking at her watch. "I already played our favorite party songs CD."

"So play it again," I said with a shrug. "Nobody will know it was already on!"

"Good thinking," Mandy said. "Wait—here comes someone! Hold on, correct that. Here comes a whole *bunch* of people!"

I looked toward the door. Ken, Aaron, and Peter had just arrived. "Hey, you guys!"

Ken looked around. "Cool—I love casino games! Where do I buy chips?"

"Right here!" Ellen called out. She patted the table by the door, where her money box was stored. "Come on in and let's get the chips moving!"

Aaron rubbed his palms together. "I feel lucky tonight." He smiled at me. "This is a great idea, Jessica, having a fund-raiser for the Child Care Center."

I shrugged, trying to look modest. "It was a good idea, wasn't it?"

Lila cleared her throat loudly. "Yeah. Good thing *Mandy* thought of it."

"But I'm the one who *gave* her the idea," I protested. "I sparked her imagination." I was about to mention my nightmare when I noticed the steady stream of kids coming down the hallway toward the playroom. "In here, everyone!" I shouted. "Get your poker chips!"

I hurried over to the slot machine and gathered the bucket of fake silver quarters. "Come on, Aaron—try this first!" I called.

"Just one second—I have to check something out," Aaron said. He went back into the hallway with Ken. Each of them was clutching a bag of poker chips.

"Where are you guys going?" I demanded, rushing over to them.

"Oh, uh . . . nowhere," Aaron said, looking uncomfortable.

I frowned. What was the deal with being so secretive? Then it hit me. "The bathrooms are actually downstairs, in the front of the building," I said softly.

Ken looked at me and shrugged. "We're not looking for the bathroom."

"You're not? Then what are you doing?" Weren't they excited to be at my party? "Don't you guys want to strike while the . . . chips are down?" Aaron blinked, looking perplexed. "No, that's not right. I mean, don't you want to strike while the . . . winning's easy? While the cards are hot? While the night is young, the dice are rolling, and—"

"Jessica! There's a line at the slot machine and you have all the tokens!" Kimberly yelled, interrupting me.

I glanced once more at Aaron and Ken as they ambled down the hall. "Just don't go into the backyard!" I called to them. Then I rushed over to the slot machine and held the basket out to the kids waiting in line. "OK! Three chances each! Who's going to hit the jackpot?"

"Come on. One more chance," Todd begged.

"Well . . . OK," I said. "But don't tell anyone. You're only supposed to get five throws for a dollar." I handed him his sixth dart.

Todd stepped back, carefully aiming his throw. So far, only Winston Egbert had managed to pop a balloon. Funny, since he's one of the most uncoordinated people I know. "Here he goes . . . for the championship!" Todd flung the dart straight at a red balloon.

The dart hit the wall and clattered onto the ground.

"Another dollar, maybe?" I suggested.

"Well, since it's for a good cause and everything," Todd said in a serious voice. Then he grinned at me. "Plus I hate losing!"

While Todd took aim at the next balloon, I glanced over at Mary, who was working at the Test Your Strength! game across the way. Kids were lined up, waiting to hit a scale with a giant wooden hammer. The game looked as though it had been used at Sweet Valley Middle School fairs for at least forty years, if not more!

Mary waved to me, then took a few steps closer and pulled a wad of dollar bills out of her pocket. "Check it out!" she said, pointing to the money. "Look how much we've raised already! And look how many people are here!"

"I know!" I called back. I'd counted at least seventy people in the backyard, and it was only eight o'clock. "The Center's going to get a complete overhaul!" Just then, I saw Peter DeHaven and Bruce Patman heading into the Child Care Center. "Uh—excuse me, Todd," I said. "I have to make sure people don't go inside—I promised Mrs. Willard! Watch the booth for me, OK?"

I handed Todd the basket of darts and rushed across the lawn after Bruce and Peter. But I was too late—they were already going through the doors. "Wait up!" I called. "You guys—"

I yanked open the door—and heard music blaring in the hallway. I frowned. What was Mrs. Willard doing, blasting her radio? I thought she was going to stay late to catch up on her paperwor—

I stopped short in the doorway to the playroom. It was packed! Not with kids who needed day care, but with Unicorns! And their friends!

I was too shocked to move. My mouth was open, but no words were coming out. Everyone was playing different card games, and laughing, and Kimberly was dancing around, passing out cups of soda. I felt as if I had just stepped into a parallel universe.

"Jackpot!" somebody roared. Silver tokens started pouring out of a slot machine onto the floor.

"We have a jackpot!" a familiar voice cried.

Jessica. She'd actually done it. She'd actually stolen our idea. I'd tried everything to keep her from knowing about our party. And here she was—in the very same place, at the very same time! Some sister! More like a dirty rotten traitor!

I marched over to the slot machine. "You have a lot of nerve! How can you be so deceitful!"

Jessica turned around. When she saw me, her face turned pale and her mouth dropped open. "E-Elizabeth?" she stammered. "What—where—why—how—"

"My thoughts exactly!" I cried.

Thirteen

"What are *you* doing here?" I demanded. I stared at Elizabeth. "Wait—there's nothing wrong at home, is there?"

"How should I know?" Elizabeth cried. "I wasn't *at* home! And as you so obviously already know, our party is here, too!"

"Here? Where?" I looked around. "What are you talking about?"

"It's outdoors, OK?" Elizabeth replied, clenching her hands into fists. She looked like she was about to punch me. She's never done that, but I took a step backward, just in case.

"Excuse me, but what have we here? A refugee from a boring party?" Kimberly asked, striding over.

"Kimberly, you are not going to believe this," I said. "Elizabeth says that the Angels' party is actually *here*—outside!"

"What?" Kimberly cried, her eyes flashing. "But that's impossible! That's preposterous! That's—hey, wait a second—you stole our idea!"

"What in the world is this?" Evie was standing in the doorway, her jaw slack. She ran over. "How could you guys just steal our idea?"

"What exactly *is* your idea?" I asked, putting my hands on my hips. "Did you guys just plan to bring everyone over here once you found out where our party was?"

"No," Elizabeth said, her blue-green eyes blazing with anger. "We planned our party here a couple of days ago. You can ask Mrs. Willard if you don't believe me."

"Fine," I said, folding my arms across my chest. "I will."

"*We* asked Mrs. Willard to have our party here—what were you doing, hiding in the broom closet?" Kimberly demanded.

"Of course not! We didn't need to steal your idea, because we had our own!" Evie insisted.

"Yeah—to have the barbecue at our house!" I cried, throwing up my hands. "That's what Todd told me yesterday!"

"Oh, yeah?" Elizabeth cried. "Well, I only *told* Todd to tell you that because I knew you'd try to find out about our party through him!"

"What? You mean you set me up?" I couldn't believe it. How could my sister deliberately try to make a fool of me?

"Yes, I set you up," Elizabeth spat out. "And I'll

do it again if I ever get the chance! Come on, Evie—
let's get back to our party." She turned and strode
toward the door.

I stared after my sister. "Oh, yeah? Well, we'll
still have a better party!" I cried.

Then I looked around the room. Were there as
many people at our casino night as there were outside? What if people thought the Angels' party was
cooler? What was going to happen to the Unicorns'
reputation? "Kimberly, we have a disaster on our
hands," I mumbled.

"No, we don't," Kimberly declared. "Because
I'm going outside right now to tell people they
ought to be in here!" She marched out the door.

Lila came running over with Ellen right behind
her. "Did I just see you talking to Elizabeth?" Lila
demanded.

"Did their party wash out or something?" Ellen
asked. "Is that why she's crashing ours?"

"Yes and no," I replied bitterly. "Elizabeth is
here. And so are the Angels." I took a deep breath.
"And so is their party."

"What?" both Ellen and Lila cried at once.

"Follow me," I said and led the way into the hallway and toward the back door. Then, propping it
open, I gazed out onto the lawn. Several dozen kids
were milling around fair games and booths, talking
and laughing. I tried to do a quick head count.

"I don't believe it," Ellen whispered.

"I *do*," Lila retorted. "Of all the nerve! Well, we
just have to make sure we have more people at our

party! Hey, why don't you put out the snacks you brought, Jessica? Once people see we have good food, they'll definitely stay."

"Sure, I'll put them out. Where are they?" I asked as we walked back inside.

"You're the one who brought them—how should I know?" Lila flicked a strand of hair out of her eyes.

I frowned. *I brought them? Since when was I supposed to bring anything?* Then I remembered that fleeting feeling I'd had in the limo on the way over. Like I was forgetting something. Only I hadn't realized that it was anything as major as *food*. For a hundred people!

"Wait a second. You didn't *forget* that you were supposed to take care of the food, did you?" Lila asked. "You said you would that day we were planning everything at Kimberly's, and—"

"Don't get hysterical. Of course I didn't forget," I said quickly. I hadn't forgotten—not exactly. How can you forget something that you never remember hearing in the first place? "I'll . . . go into the kitchen right now and get them."

I rushed out of the playroom, even though I knew I wouldn't find any snacks in the kitchen— except maybe some leftover animal crackers and peanut butter that Mrs. Willard had bought for the kids. How I could possibly have missed something as crucial as snacks? I live for snacks! I felt like kicking myself. Then again, I figured, I could wait until Kimberly took responsibility for *that*.

*   *   *

"So they're in there? Right now?" Maria asked.

I nodded. I was still recovering from the shock of seeing Jessica and a full-blown party when I'd expected to see an empty room. I couldn't find the words to describe how angry and let down I felt. "We planned everything perfectly. How did it go so wrong?" I wondered out loud.

"I don't know, but what are we going to do about it?" Mary asked. "Look at Kimberly over there—probably bribing everyone to go inside."

Maria rolled her eyes. "No way. She wouldn't settle for bribing. That's too *good* for her. She's probably threatening them instead!"

Ken walked over. "Excuse me, Elizabeth? Is there some soda around here?"

"Soda?" I repeated.

"Sure, we have lots of soda. You brought it, remember?" Evie said, smiling at me.

I swallowed hard. I'd been so caught up in worrying about our party and daydreaming about Todd and being angry at Jessica—I'd completely forgotten that I'd promised to bring bottles of soda and juice to the party! We'd worked so hard to get all these people to come . . . and now they were going to be dying of thirst, all thanks to me!

"Want me to help you carry some bottles?" Mary offered. "There's nobody waiting at my booth right now, so—"

"No!" I cried. "I mean, uh, that's OK. I can get it myself. I, umm . . . stuck it in the fridge when we got here."

"But Mrs. Willard said we weren't supposed to go in there," Evie protested, looking concerned.

"It's OK!" I said. "She cleared a path for me."

I hurried away toward the Child Care Center building, praying there was some leftover juice or something in the refrigerator.

If not, I would have to run to the nearest convenience store—and that was three miles away!

I reached into the cabinet and felt around for a box, a bag . . . even a crumb would help at this point. The kitchen area was completely dark. I didn't want to turn on the light and run the risk of someone seeing that I had no idea where the snacks were.

At least Kimberly had remembered to bring the beverages. In fact, she was going to be pointing that out to me for the rest of my life. I could hear her now: "Some of us remember our responsibilities. Some of us care about our club!"

I stopped as I heard footsteps behind me. A second later, the refrigerator door opened. Great. Kimberly was probably getting more soda. I needed an excuse, fast—something involving boys and how they always steal food.

I slowly turned to face Kimberly. But in the light shining out of the refrigerator into the darkness, I didn't see Kimberly. I saw Elizabeth, who had her hands around one of *our* bottles of soda!

I narrowed my eyes. "Oh, and I suppose stealing our party plan wasn't enough—now you're stealing our soda, too!" I cried.

Elizabeth was so startled, she dropped the plastic bottle and it bounced on the floor.

"Great. Now we can't even open it without making a total mess," I complained. "You probably can't wait to see me go back to my party with cola splattered all over me! Since you love humiliating me so much!"

Elizabeth gasped. "*I* love humiliating *you*? Oh, that's a good one! You're the one who decided to have your party on the same night as I did. Just so nobody would come to mine and you could look better than me!" Her eyes were shining with tears.

"I only did that because you and the rest of the Angels have this attitude like you're so superior to us!" I cried, my lip quivering.

"We act like we're superior to you? Are you serious?" Elizabeth looked appalled. "You're the one who called my club boring and goody-goody!"

"So? That's nothing!" I fumed. "You called *us* nasty and unfair!"

Suddenly the overhead light went on. Mrs. Willard strode into the kitchen, her hands on her hips. "Girls! I could hear you in my office! What's the problem?"

I pointed at Elizabeth. "She is!"

Elizabeth pointed at me. "Her!"

Mrs. Willard shook her head and sighed, sounding completely exasperated. "I'm listening to you, but what I hear sounds more like something I'd hear from the five-year-olds I take care of every day! Can't you talk about your problems in a way more mature than just standing here pointing fingers and blaming each other?"

I stared at the floor. I did feel kind of ridiculous, now that Mrs. Willard mentioned it. "But Mrs. Willard, we were supposed to have our party here," I protested.

"And you are," Mrs. Willard said. "So what's the problem?"

Elizabeth looked confused. "But . . . well, *we* were supposed to have *our* party here."

Mrs. Willard sighed. "Yes, indeed. You both spoke to me about having your parties here, and here you are."

I frowned. "You mean the Angels talked to you, too? Why didn't you tell us?"

"Yeah," Elizabeth added. "Why did you agree to have both parties here at the same time?"

Mrs. Willard let out her breath in another long sigh. "Because, silly me . . . I thought that *maybe*, just maybe, if you all got together in one place, you'd see how ridiculous this little club feud has gotten. And you'd realize that having separate parties is foolish when you can all get along like civilized people! Of course, if even twin sisters can't be civilized to each other . . ." Mrs. Willard shook her head. "I suppose I was giving you too much credit."

I bit my lip. I hate when adults tell me that. Most of the time, they don't give me *enough* credit, as far as I'm concerned. But somehow what Mrs. Willard said made sense—a little bit of sense, anyway. Maybe our club feud had gotten kind of out of control. Maybe I shouldn't have pretended to be Elizabeth in front of Todd. And maybe I shouldn't have said those mean things about how Todd wouldn't go to her party.

I took a deep breath. "Elizabeth, I'm sorry," I said in low voice. I *was* sorry, but I didn't want anyone else who happened to pass by the kitchen to hear me say so. "I shouldn't have done some of the stuff I did. I got kind of carried away, I guess."

Elizabeth smiled timidly. "I'm sorry, too. We shouldn't have planned both our parties for the same weekend in the first place."

"Yes, you should have," Mrs. Willard said. "Because the Center really needs the money!" She laughed. "But maybe you should have channeled some of those charitable feelings toward each other?" She raised one eyebrow, giving us this very critical look that was kind of funny, too.

"It's not too late," Elizabeth said. "I mean, we could still have our parties together. Since we are in the same place and all."

I grinned. "Yeah, why not? After all, we've never been to a party without each other."

"And that way we can pool our resources, right?" Elizabeth asked. Her face turned slightly pink.

"What do you mean?" I asked.

"Well, I . . . see, I . . . forgot that, well, that I was supposed to bring the soda," Elizabeth managed to say. "So that's why I was in here, rummaging around for some. Do you think if we join our parties, we could have some of your beverages?"

"Geez, I don't know, Elizabeth," I said, putting on my most serious-looking frown. "Sharing our drinks with you—that's kind of a serious step. I don't know how the other Unicorns would feel about that."

"Oh." Elizabeth's face fell.

"However." I tapped my finger against the counter. "If, perhaps, you guys had a couple of bags of chips to trade for some soda—"

"Sure!" Elizabeth burst out eagerly.

"And maybe some sandwiches and cookies and popcorn—you know, enough for, say, a hundred people—"

A huge smile spread across Elizabeth's face. "You forgot to bring the food, didn't you?" she cried. "That's why you were in here, looking in the cabinets!"

I bit my lip. As long as Elizabeth and I were going to be best friends again, there was no need to keep secrets. I nodded slowly. "You know what? I don't even remember saying I'd bring them!" I confessed.

"I was so busy trying to fool you, I completely forgot that people need things to drink at parties," Elizabeth said with a giggle.

Then we both burst out laughing.

"You're identical, all right," Mrs. Willard commented. "You've got identical amnesia!"

"Come on," I said, taking Elizabeth's arm. "Let's get back to our parties—party, I mean!"

Fourteen

"Come on, you guys. It's the only way," I pleaded.

"Have you lost your mind?" Kimberly turned to Lila. "Has she lost her mind?"

The five of us were standing in a close huddle in the middle of the dance floor. Around us, everyone was laughing and gambling and dancing and having a great time . . . even if they were a little on the hungry side.

"We have to combine our party with the Angels'," I declared for what had to be the tenth time.

Lila took a step closer to me and peered into my eyes. "Are you totally losing it? Do you hear the sound of the slot machine bell ringing in your ears?"

"No!" I cried. "I'm serious. Look, I know it's horrible that I forgot the food, but this is the only solution. The Angels have tons of snacks. And Elizabeth would be happy to share them with us, only they want some of our soda. Is that so hard to understand?"

"I think it sounds fine," Mandy said with a shrug. "And that way, if we just keep the back door open, people can go back and forth between both parties without a big hassle."

"But you're missing the point. We don't *want* them to go back and forth," Kimberly argued. "We want them to stay right here!"

"Look, they're going back and forth whether we want them to or not." I pointed at Ken and Aaron. "Those guys have been in and out of here three times already."

"The longer we stand here arguing, the more irritated people are going to get," Ellen admitted, looking around. "They're waiting for us to deal the cards and spin the wheel and all that. We might be losing money!"

"Not to mention guests," Mandy commented, pointing to Jake Hamilton and Charlie Cashman, who were headed for the front door.

Lila looked at her watch. "Well, it's already nine. We only have one more hour. I *guess* it would be OK. Just don't expect me to be happy about it!"

"People *have* been mentioning to me that they're hungry," Kimberly mused. "Thanks to you, Jessica."

"I'm sorry, OK? I'm really, really sorry," I said, rolling my eyes. "It's not the end of the world!"

"When we have to join up with the Angels just to have food at our party? If that isn't the end of the world, I don't know what is," Kimberly grumbled. She let out an exasperated sigh. "Oh, all right. Put our extra soda out there. I have to get back to the poker table."

She walked off, Lila and Ellen close behind her.

I looked at Mandy and grinned. "This is the only way, you know."

Mandy giggled. "To tell you the truth, I'm kind of glad you forgot the food. I wanted to go to both parties, anyway!"

I straightened the stack of napkins on the table. "That should do it, right?" I asked Mandy. She'd managed to sneak away from the Unicorns to help me set up the refreshments.

"Chips, cookies, and soda, at the exact midway point." Mandy brushed a crumb off the table. "I don't see how anyone could complain about that." She put her finger to her lips, looking thoughtful. "But they *will* complain, of course. They'll be out here measuring inches and centimeters, just to make sure it's halfway between both parties."

I laughed. "Thanks a lot for helping!"

Mandy shrugged. "No problem." She grabbed a cookie off the table. "Well, I'd better get back inside before somebody steals all my chips. Poker chips, that is." She winked at me and rushed back inside the building.

"What's all this?"

I turned around. Todd was standing behind me. I'd talked to him a dozen times that night, but my heart started pounding as if I was seeing him for the first time. He was really friendly and every-thing, but I still couldn't tell if he liked me the same way I liked him.

"How come you moved everything?" he asked.

"It's kind of a long story," I told him, trying to breathe normally. "But basically, we decided to share some of our stuff. It's actually my fault." I wrinkled my nose. "I forgot that I was supposed to bring stuff to drink."

"Really? What are you, a camel?" Todd laughed.

I giggled nervously. "What can I say? I guess I've had a lot on my mind," I admitted. Like him, for instance.

"Like fooling Jessica?" Todd smiled mischie-vously. "Or does the fact that you're sharing food mean you guys are on speaking terms again?"

I nodded. "Yeah, fortunately. Not that it wasn't fun fooling her yesterday!"

"It was," Todd agreed. "I'd definitely do that again, if you want. Even if it didn't work out, we still make a great team."

We, I thought. He'd actually referred to us as *we.* Like we were a couple!

Before I could say anything, Todd reached out and took my hand. "Hey, let's get out of here for a second."

I almost keeled over. Did this mean what I thought it did? Todd and I were holding hands— right in front of everyone! As much as I wanted to take off with him, though, I couldn't desert my friends. "I'd love to—but I probably shouldn't leave my own party," I told him.

"Don't worry—we're not leaving. We're just moving a little bit," Todd said. He led me through the crowd over to the jungle gym. "Kind of quiet over here, isn't it?"

I leaned back against a rung. "It's nice."

"Yeah." Todd sighed. "It's nice to be . . . you know, just the two of us."

"Yeah." The word came out as a squeak. "It is." I looked up at Todd. He was looking at me. And before I knew what was happening, he leaned over and kissed me!

I felt like I was about to melt. Could my night work out any more perfectly?

"OK, Elizabeth. Have you been holding out on us or what?" Mary asked me as I walked over to her booth at the end of the night.

I handed her the envelope full of cash I'd collected for the darts game. "Here's the money. I'm not holding out on you."

Mary put her hands on her hips. "I'm not talking about *money*, silly. I'm talking about you and Todd!"

I felt my neck prickle. "What do you mean?"

Maria came up behind Mary. "Did you ask her yet?"

"Ask me?" I laughed nervously.

"So are you and Todd a major item or what?" Evie demanded, hurrying over.

"Shhh!" I whispered.

"Oh, like it's any secret," Mary said, rolling her

eyes. "You guys were only holding hands fifteen minutes ago—in front of everyone!"

"We were? I mean, well, yeah, we were," I admitted. "But that doesn't mean anything."

"It doesn't?" Maria looked confused.

I felt myself start to blush. A part of me was dying to tell them about what had happened between me and Todd, but I didn't want them to think I'd gone all boy-crazy—especially not now after all we'd been through with the Unicorns. The Angels depended on me. I couldn't let them down. "No . . . we're just friends," I told them.

Evie nodded. "Uh-huh. And I suppose people who are just friends *kiss* all the time."

"What? How did you know?" I cried. I thought Todd and I were hidden in the darkness.

Evie grinned sheepishly. "I didn't mean to look, but I saw you guys."

I let out all my breath. "Well, I guess there's no use pretending anymore. It's true. I like Todd. I like him a lot." I looked down at my hands. "I'm sorry if that makes me more like a Unicorn, and I hope you guys will forgive me, but I can't help it—I just like him!"

Maria, Mary, and Evie all looked at each other with very serious expressions.

This is it, I thought. *They're going to tell me that I'm not acting like an Angel, that I'm as boy-crazy as Jessica ever was, maybe even more.*

Then Maria burst out laughing. "Like we care!"

Mary put her arm around my shoulder.

"Actually, we *do* care. We think it's awesome!"

"You do?" I couldn't believe it.

"Of course. We just wish you'd let us in on your little secret crush earlier!" Evie said. "That way, who knows? Maybe we could all have gotten dates for tonight."

"So . . . you don't think I'm being silly?" I asked, looking around at them.

"If kissing Todd Wilkins is silly, then . . . I hope I'm that silly someday," Mary declared. She held up her hands. "Not that I'm interested in Todd! He's just cute, that's all."

"Not as cute as Peter DeHaven," Evie said, gazing wistfully across the backyard.

"Please, nobody ranks up there with Bruce Patman," Maria said dreamily.

I laughed. I had a feeling the Angels would never be the same again!

"Attention, everyone! Can I have your attention?" Mrs. Willard rapped a huge plastic mallet against the counter in the playroom. "I have an announcement to make!"

I dropped the last slot machine token into the bucket and looked up at Mrs. Willard. I'd been hoping I'd have a chance to play it once everyone left, but it was ten o'clock and no one had left yet! In just a few minutes, Mr. Fowler and Charles were coming to pick everything up.

"I'd like to thank you all so very much for coming tonight. Your support means a lot to me—and to all the people who use the Sweet Valley Child Care Center!" Mrs. Willard said. Her eyes were shining as if she was about to start crying.

Man. I never thought Mrs. Willard was so emotional. It was obvious that the Center meant everything to her. I have to admit, I was getting a little choked up, too, just thinking of all the kids I'd helped.

"Thanks to the Angels and the Unicorns, we've raised enough money tonight to make a serious dent in all the repair work the Center needs," Mrs. Willard continued. "So let's hear it for the Unicorn Club and the Angels!"

Everyone started applauding. Mandy stepped into the center of the playroom and took a big bow. "Thank you, thank you."

Peter DeHaven threw a plastic cup at her. Mandy laughed.

"I'm sure you'll all agree with me that their *combined* effort has made a real difference tonight!" Mrs. Willard said, smiling at me. "Thanks, girls!"

"You're welcome!" I called over the crowd toward her.

"Well, I still say we brought in more money than the Angels," Kimberly declared. She and Lila were standing behind me.

"No doubt," Lila agreed. "I did a count at one point, and there were a hundred and one people in here, and only ninety-eight out there."

"Exactly," Kimberly said.

I turned around. "You guys, don't you want to just relax and have *fun* at some point?"

Lila sniffed. "I *am* having fun. Much more fun than the Angels, I'm sure."

"And who knows what would have happened if we'd had our own *food*," Kimberly added pointedly.

I rolled my eyes. As far as I was concerned, the night had been a total success. If I hadn't forgotten the snacks, I wouldn't have bumped into Elizabeth in the kitchen and we'd probably still be feuding. It was almost lucky. And we'd made so much money for the Center, I wouldn't have to clean out that filthy sink again!

There was only one problem, as far as I could see. A part of me *did* still want to prove that the Unicorns were the number-one club at school.

But it was only Friday night, I told myself. We had the rest of the weekend to come up with another plan.

And one thing was for sure, I thought, looking over at Elizabeth, who was holding Todd's hand and gazing up into his eyes. Whatever our next plan was, Todd Wilkins would definitely *not* be involved!

I reached into the bucket and tried to pick the perfect silver token. For some reason, after everything that had happened, I was feeling incredibly lucky.

I slipped a token into the slot machine and slowly pulled the lever. I stared as the dials spun around.

Cherry . . . cherry . . .

Lemon.

Oh, well. Two out of three isn't bad.

Then I grabbed another token. After all, the night wasn't over *yet*.

"So did you hit the jackpot?" Ellen asked me toward the end of the evening. We were both standing by the refreshment table. I cringed. Losing is bad enough, but admitting defeat is even worse. "That's not important," I replied briskly. "What matters is that we raised a ton of money for the Child Care Center."

Ellen's eyes twinkled. "Yeah. Now the kids will have *plenty* of graham crackers. They'll be so psyched." She frowned. "By the way, what *is* it about kids and graham crackers? What's so great about them, anyway?"

"It's a little-kid thing," I told her authoritatively. I decided not to mention that I like graham crackers a lot, too. "If you were more in touch with the kids, you'd understand."

Ellen looked offended. "I know how to take care of kids as well as any of you guys!"

How well do the Unicorns know how to take care of kids? Find out in THE UNICORN CLUB #12, **Five Girls and a Baby.**

SIGN UP FOR THE SWEET VALLEY HIGH® FAN CLUB!

Hey, girls! Get all the gossip on Sweet Valley High's® most popular teenagers when you join our fantastic Fan Club! As a member, you'll get all of this really cool stuff:

- Membership Card with your own personal Fan Club ID number
- A Sweet Valley High® Secret Treasure Box
- Sweet Valley High® Stationery
- Official Fan Club Pencil (for secret note writing!)
- Three Bookmarks
- A "Members Only" Door Hanger
- Two Skeins of J. & P. Coats® Embroidery Floss with flower barrette instruction leaflet
- Two editions of *The Oracle* newsletter
- Plus exclusive Sweet Valley High® product offers, special savings, contests, and much more!

- -

Be the first to find out what Jessica & Elizabeth Wakefield are up to by joining the Sweet Valley High® Fan Club for the one-year membership fee of only $6.25 each for U.S. residents, $8.25 for Canadian residents (U.S. currency). Includes shipping & handling.

Send a check or money order (do not send cash) made payable to "Sweet Valley High® Fan Club" along with this form to:

SWEET VALLEY HIGH® FAN CLUB, BOX 3919-B, SCHAUMBURG, IL 60168-3919

NAME ___Vanessa Milara___
(Please print clearly)

ADDRESS ___112 Charlotte Terr.___

CITY ___Roselle Park___ STATE ___NJ___ ZIP ___07204___
(Required)

AGE ___10___ BIRTHDAY ___04 / 09 / 86___

Offer good while supplies last. Allow 6-8 weeks after check clearance for delivery. Addresses without ZIP codes cannot be honored. Offer good in USA & Canada only. Void where prohibited by law.

©1993 by Francine Pascal   LCI-1383-123